Dear Reader,

Wedding bells, orange blossom, blushing brides and dashing grooms...and happy ever after? As we all know, the path of true love often doesn't run smoothly—both before and after the knot is tied. So what makes two people's love for each other special? And why can love survive everything that is thrown at it?

In these two linked books I've explored that very thing—how one couple copes with a tragedy that has the potential to destroy their marriage; and, in the second book, how that same disaster sends out ripples of bitterness and disillusionment toward their friend, tarnishing his view of love until...

Well, read the books and all will be revealed! I've thoroughly enjoyed writing them, and do hope you enjoy reading them.

Love,

Helen Brooks

HELEN BROOKS

Husband by Contract

Harlequin Books

TORONTO • NEW YORK • LONDON
AMSTERDAM • PARIS • SYDNEY • HAMBURG
STOCKHOLM • ATHENS • TOKYO • MILAN
MADRID • WARSAW • BUDAPEST • AUCKLAND

ISBN 0-373-11934-8

HUSBAND BY CONTRACT

First North American Publication 1998.

Copyright © 1997 by Helen Brooks.

This edition published by arrangement with Harlequin Books S.A.

® and TM are trademarks of the publisher. Trademarks indicated with
® are registered in the United States Patent and Trademark Office, the
Canadian Trade Marks Office and in other countries.

Printed in U.S.A.

CHAPTER ONE

'EXCUSE me, but are you feeling all right?'

'I'm sorry?' Grace felt as though she had just returned from a dark, cold place as she focused her deep blue eyes on the concerned face of the stewardess bending over her, the gentle murmur of conversation from the other passengers on the plane penetrating the horror that had held her in its grip. 'Oh, yes, yes, thank you, I'm fine.' The pretty young face watching her didn't look convinced and she added quickly, 'A headache. I've had a headache all day, that's all.'

'Oh, you should have said.' The tall, slim stewardess smiled her professional smile of sympathy as she straightened. 'I'll get you a couple of aspirin, shall I?'

'Thank you.' Grace nodded her appreciation. 'If it's no trouble,' she added quietly, forcing a smile from somewhere.

A headache. If only this fear and panic that had made eating and sleeping impossible since she had received the telegram could be dealt with as easily as a headache. The flat formality of the printed words swam into her mind again as her stomach churned.

I have been instructed by Donato Vittoria to inform you of the sudden death of his mother, and to request your presence at the funeral on 23rd April. The service will be held at the Church of the Madonna di Mezz' Loreto at midday.

That had been all. No explanation, no suggestion that she call or contact the family in any way, just a cold, terse announcement from the Vittorias' solicitor, Signor Fellini.

But it hadn't really been an announcement, had it? she

5

thought sickly. It was a demand, a decree, by the autocratic head of the Vittoria clan, whose word was law and
power absolute. *Donato*. Oh, God, I shan't be able to
stand it, she prayed desperately; help me get through the
next few days. . .

'Here we are.' Again the smooth, pleasant voice of
the stewardess brought her back from the edge of despair
and into the real world as she handed Grace a glass of
water and the aspirin. 'Not long now and we'll be landing; you'll feel better then,' she added brightly, the tone
faintly patronising.

'Thank you.' Grace obediently swallowed both the
aspirin and the water and settled back in her seat as
she closed her eyes. She knew what the stewardess was
thinking; it had been transparently obvious. Poor little
thing, she's frightened of flying. Well, she was frightened
all right, absolutely terrified, but not of flying.

Oh, she had to pull herself together, she told herself
angrily. She was a grown woman of twenty-three, not
some nervous, over-excited schoolgirl who couldn't say
boo to a goose. If only she looked her twenty-three years,
that would give her a little more confidence for the days
ahead, but her petite five feet four inches added to red-
gold curls that defied all efforts at smoothness and a
naturally elfin face took at least five years off her age
despite her careful choice of clothes.

But she was old inside. She shuddered, her hands
clenching on her lap. Ancient, antediluvian inside. More
than old enough to cope with Donato and the rest of the
Vittoria family.

That thought carried her through the rest of the journey
and the arrival at Naples airport, and once through
Customs she collected the one suitcase she had brought
with her and prepared to find a taxi, her face white and
strained and her small, slim body held erect amidst all
the bustle and chaos around her.

'Grace.' She froze for an infinitesimal moment, mind
and body registering the shock of hearing that deep, cool
voice with its heavy Italian accent speaking her name,

and then forced herself to turn slowly as she took a long, steadying breath.

'Donato.' A smile was beyond her as she took in the tall, dark man watching her so closely, his black eyes narrowed in the tanned hardness of his face and his firm, sensual mouth unsmiling like hers. He was still the same! She felt her heart begin to slam against her ribcage with the force of a sledge-hammer and willed the panic to cease. She had to be in control, give the impression of calm and cold restraint; anything else would be seized upon as weakness and used against her. 'I'm very sorry about your mother,' she said quietly, hoping the slight quiver in her voice would pass unnoticed. 'She was a truly great lady.'

'Yes, she was.' He was standing very still, his loose-fitting trousers and dark blue cotton shirt immaculate as always and sitting on the big, lithe body in a way guaranteed to make any female heart beat a little faster.

But not hers. Grace took another hidden breath before she spoke. Definitely not hers, never again. 'The telegram said it was sudden?' she asked carefully, keeping her voice neutral. His had been quite expressionless, cold and flat.

'A haemorrhage, in the brain.' He touched his forehead as he spoke, the movement emphasising the heavy gold watch on his wrist and the thick gold band on the third finger of his left hand. 'She knew nothing about it. Now. . .' He turned slightly, gesturing to someone behind him. 'Antonio will take your bags——'

'I'm not staying at Casa Pontina!' She had spoken too sharply and too quickly but it was too late to try and moderate her tone as the handsome male face in front of her darkened. 'I. . . I've made arrangements,' she said hastily. 'It's all taken care of.' How had he known of her arrival? Why was he here? What was all this in aid of? As the numbing shock of the sudden encounter began to fade Grace found a barrage of questions attacking her mind.

'Where else would you stay but at Casa Pontina?' The

arrogance was pure Vittoria and as such hit her on the raw, causing her soft mouth to tighten in response to the challenge.

'I'm booked in at the Hotel La Pergola,' she said coldly, 'for three nights.'

'I think not.' He smiled now, but it didn't touch the glittering blackness of his eyes. 'It would not be fitting in the circumstances and this you know. It will be expected that you stay at Casa Pontina.'

He spoke as if the matter were settled, and as the uniformed chauffeur reached for her case again at Donato's tight nod she found herself whisking it behind her and stepping back a pace. 'I don't have to do what is expected of me, not any more,' she said fiercely. 'I'm answerable to myself and no one else. You can't order me about like you do everyone else.'

'Everyone, Grace?' The dark voice was quiet and silky now, with a thread of steel that she knew was meant to intimidate. 'I had forgotten how you like to exaggerate.'

'That doesn't surprise me,' she tossed back bitterly. 'I'm only surprised you remember my name.'

'Oh, I remember your name, *mia piccola*.' The soft endearment hit her like a punch in the chest and it took all of her will-power not to let it show. 'I remember everything about you. Now, you *will* let Antonio take your luggage,' he continued in a smooth, conversational tone of voice that was belied by the glittering intensity in his eyes, 'and you *will* stay at Casa Pontina.'

'Why should I?' she asked hotly, her blue eyes stormy.

'Because it is what my mother would have wanted.'

She stared at him, the anger and bitter resentment draining away as the truth in his words left her pale and shaking. Liliana *would* have wanted her to stay at the family home, she acknowledged painfully. In fact the matriarch of the Vittoria clan would have been horrified at anything else.

This was one last thing she could do for Liliana, she thought sadly, for the tall, proud, aristocratic Italian woman who had wielded such power and influence within her own family and shown Grace nothing but love and kindness from their first meeting. Yes, she would do this for Liliana; for Liliana she would even endure living under the same roof as Donato for three days and nights.

'Very well.' She saw the flash of triumph in the jet-black eyes and had to bite her lip to prevent more hot words. Liliana was dead, the last tentative link with Italy was broken by her demise, and she would endeavour to see out this final travesty with the sort of dignity and aplomb that the genteel Italian woman would have expected from her. 'I shall have to cancel my reservation at La Pergola on the way to Casa Pontina.'

'*Sì*, of course; this will be no problem.' The words were smooth and self-satisfied and caused her stomach muscles to tighten.

Donato nodded in a sharp little bow, clicking his fingers at Antonio, who reached behind her for the case, his pock-marked face beneath its chauffeur's cap of blue and gold apologetic. '*Scusi, signora.*' The voice was humble, the appearance of the big, beefy individual anything but.

Antonio might not know any English, Grace reflected with a touch of wryness, but he had certainly had no trouble in following the general theme of the conversation.

She had always thought Donato's chauffeur resembled a member of the Sicilian mafia rather than a household servant, and this idea was reinforced now as she followed the swarthy, dark figure out to the Vittoria Mercedes, Donato's hand at her elbow, feeling for all the world as though she was being led to her execution.

The fifty-or-so-mile drive to Donato's magnificent villa in Sorrento would be no problem——the Mercedes' excellent air conditioning added to the fact that the late-April temperature was only just touching seventy degrees made travelling at midday still a pleasure, unlike in high summer——but sitting in close proximity to Donato for well over an hour was a different matter.

Grace had planned to stay overnight in Naples and

travel down to Sorrento early the next morning by hire
car in time for the funeral, returning the same day. That
would have meant she could have paid her last respects
to Liliana while retaining some degree of independence,
but. . .she might have known Donato would overrule any
arrangements she had made.

Donato opened the car door for her but she paused
before sliding in, looking up into his cold, handsome
face as she asked, 'How did you know I was coming
today, and on that flight?'

'Does it matter?' His voice was cool and dismissive,
his manner remote. It was an attitude she had seen him
adopt many times in the past and it usually had the
desired effect of forestalling further conversation, but not
so with her, and not today.

'Yes, it does, to me.' She continued to hold his glance,
her vivid blue eyes with their thick, curling lashes dark
with determination. 'I wasn't aware I told anyone of
my plans.'

'Possibly not,' he said.

'Well, then?' Her gaze was becoming a glare but she
couldn't do anything about it; his arrogance was bringing
up a strong feeling of rebellion. 'How did you know?'
she asked again.

'I know most things about you, Grace.' The way he
said her name still had the power to make her weak but
she would rather have walked through coals of fire than
admit it, even to herself.

'Meaning?' she snapped tightly, her eyes hot.

'You want me to list all the things I know about you?'
he asked smoothly, with simulated surprise. 'Here?
Where we could so easily be overheard?'

'Stop playing games, Donato.' She said it with a touch
of weariness that narrowed his eyes on the whiteness
of her face, in which exhaustion was suddenly all too
evident.

'Is that what you think I am doing, *mia piccola*?' he
said softly. 'Playing the game? Nothing could be further
from the truth.' For a moment something fierce and hot

blazed in the heavily lashed black eyes but then his lids shuttered the fire as he half turned from her, gesturing into the car. 'Get in and I will tell you what you wish to know.'

She got in—there was really little else she could do after all, she told herself flatly—and when he joined her a moment later on the spacious back seat, and her senses caught a whiff of the familiar aftershave he had specially made for him, the wickedly blended allure of spices and lemon and something indefinable made her nerve-ends jump. How many nights had she spent locked in his arms, she asked herself tremulously, breathing in that heady fragrance after hours of mad, passionate love? Hours that had sent her up to the heights, hours that had had her begging, pleading for sweet relief and then barely able to stand the ecstasy when he had obliged.

She had thought then that they would be together for the rest of their lives, that nothing in this world or the one beyond could possibly separate them, that they were two halves of one glorious whole. But she had learnt. . . Her mouth tightened and she breathed deeply through her nostrils. Oh, how she had learnt.

'Well?' She forced her face to remain blank as she turned slightly, although his nearness sent her heart flickering into her throat. 'How did you know I was arriving today?'

'I have been aware of all your movements in the last year, Grace,' he said calmly. 'You surely did not think it could be otherwise?'

'All of my movements?' she echoed, puzzled. 'I really don't see. . .' And then it dawned. 'You don't mean. . . You haven't had me watched?' she asked angrily, her voice and colour rising in unison. 'Is that what you're saying?'

'Of course.' He eyed her coldly, the straight line of his mouth expressing distaste at her lack of control.

'*Of course?*' Her cry of outrage made him wince slightly, but she had given up trying to maintain the new cool image; she had never been so furious in all her life.

'You dare to sit there and tell me you've been spying on me,' she hissed heatedly, 'without the slightest shred of guilt or embarrassment? How dared you do that, Donato? I can't believe even you would sink so low.'

'Careful, Grace.' He leant towards her now, his face stony and his eyes dark, glittering chips of black ice. 'I will only permit so much.'

'*You* will only permit so much?' She was quite oblivious to the big car negotiating its way out of the airport surroundings or of Antonio sitting stoically in the driving seat. The glass partition made their conversation inaudible but no one could have doubted the tenor of their exchange. 'And what about me? What about what I will permit? You tell me you've invaded my privacy, reduced me to a goldfish in a glass bowl—'

He swore, softly and vehemently in swift Italian, before growling, 'This is a ridiculous conversation and one which I have no inclination to continue. There is no question that you are the fish in the bowl.'

'But you *paid* someone to spy on me!' she spat shrilly. 'What gives you the right to think you can act like that? It's. . .it's immoral.'

'I will not discuss this with you until you can control yourself,' he said icily, 'and I have no wish to argue with you at this time, Grace. It is not fitting.'

His words brought the image of Liliana's proud, beautiful face onto the screen of her mind, and she clenched her teeth in an effort to prevent more hot accusations spilling out. She was here for his mother's funeral—she had to remember that, she told herself painfully, and if there was one thing she was sure of it was that Donato had loved Liliana dearly. But once she was back in England. . .

She bit her lip as she forced the rage to subside. There was no way she was going to let such a situation continue. For twelve months she had hesitated to proceed along the road she had chosen but now the way was clear and free of obstacles. There was no reason to vacillate any longer—she knew it in her heart—but still, still it hurt, and she was angry, *furious* with herself because of it. But this last outrage had confirmed everything. Her mouth tightened and she took a long, silent breath to ease the churning in her stomach. The die was cast.

When they arrived at the Hotel La Pergola Donato leant forward and slid the glass partition aside as Antonio brought the car to a standstill on the pebbled sweep of drive in front of the gracious building. 'Antonio will see to the cancellation,' he said over his shoulder to Grace as the powerful engine died.

'I would prefer to do it myself,' she said quickly. She had conceded to his insistence that she stay at Casa Pontina for Liliana's sake, but he might as well learn right now that she was capable of running her own life without his assistance.

'As you wish.' The voice was lazy, the expression in his eyes anything but as she climbed out of the car before Antonio could open her door and marched stiffly up the wide, curving steps and into the hotel interior without glancing back.

Once inside she paused for a moment before continuing to the massive semicircular reception desk, aware that her legs were shaking and her stomach trembling at the shock of seeing him again. 'Control, control, Grace,' she murmured quietly to herself, earning a sidelong glance from an old Italian couple who were passing. Their relationship was over, irrevocably over; he knew that as well as she did. All she had to do was get through the next day or two as best she could until she could fly home to her tiny flat and job as receptionist at the local doctors' surgery in a quiet part of Kent.

The hotel accepted her explanation that friends had picked her up from the airport and were insisting she stay with them with customary Italian good humour, and within a few minutes they were on their way again, driving deeper into the countryside where the magic of Italy reached out to touch her. She had always loved the country, from the first moment she had set foot in it five years before, as an eager eighteen-year-old desperate to prove herself in her new position as nanny to a wealthy Italian couple with two children, until the agonising parting a year ago.

She was particularly receptive to beauty, and the winding streets of terracotta-roofed stone houses, ancient gothic cathedrals and medieval fountains, poplar-shaded farmsteads surrounded by vineyards and olive groves, and the unspoilt tranquillity of the real Italy, had moved her to tears in the early days.

Sorrento, the family home of the Vittorias for centuries, was quaint, colourful and romantic, and their magnificent seventeenth-century villa, situated high above the blue waters of the Bay of Naples, had panoramic views from its wonderful old balconies bright with trailing bougainvillea. The whole area around Sorrento was a treasure trove of mythology, history and scenic splendour, and Grace had fallen deeply and hopelessly in love with it and. . .Donato.

He was a friend of the young couple whose children she had come out to nanny, and almost from their first meeting, when she had been in Italy all of two weeks, she had known she loved him. He was wildly handsome, an experienced and worldly-wise twenty-five to her innocent eighteen, and he'd swept her off her feet, utterly and completely.

How was she going to get through the next three days staying at Casa Pontina? Grace asked herself now, aware that the powerful memories the grand old house—named after the southern wind of Sorrento—was capable of evoking would not be conducive to her peace of mind.

As the oldest son Donato had inherited the villa and the Vittoria estate and businesses on his father's death just months before Grace had first come to Italy, and he ran his small empire with the help of a management team of trusted employees who were completely committed to both Donato and the Vittoria name.

Bianca, Donato's adopted sister, had married his best friend at seventeen and lived some miles away in the Sant'Agnello district of Sorrento where her husband cultivated his large crop of orange groves, although it was the Bellini business interests in Naples that had provided her husband with his vast wealth.

Although Bianca was only a month or two younger than Grace the two girls had never become friends, Bianca's jealousy and bitterness at Grace's popularity within the family remaining despite all Grace's efforts to win the beautiful Italian girl over. Bianca had particularly resented Grace's closeness to little Lorenzo, the youngest member of the Vittoria family, who had been something of a miracle baby, his parents having been told at Donato's birth that no more children were possible. He had adored Grace with the devotion of a small puppy and she had loved him right back.

'There was no problem at your hasty departure?' Donato's cool, deep voice broke into her thoughts of Lorenzo and brought her eyes to his dark profile. For a moment she thought he was referring to that other soul-searing time, so firmly had her mind retreated into the past, but then realisation dawned.

'No.' She quickly lowered her gaze; the hard-boned male face with its strong classical features and firm, sensual mouth still possessed a magnetism that was unnerving. 'Everyone was very understanding,' she said quietly.

'And Dr Penn? He too was...very understanding?' Donato asked expressionlessly without turning to glance her way.

'Jim? Yes, of course; I've said, haven't I? Everyone was very sympathetic...' Her voice trailed away and she raised her eyes to his face again but the cold façade was blank, no emotion in the stony features as he kept his gaze fixed straight ahead.

She didn't ask how he knew the individual doctors' names; no doubt his source had been very thorough, she thought tightly, but why pick Jim Penn out for special mention above the other three doctors at the busy surgery?

'This is good.' Donato's voice was smooth, too

smooth, and now he turned to her slowly, his dark eyes flashing over her pale face and his mouth twisting in a smile that was no smile at all. 'I'm sure you will be greatly missed.'

'I doubt it, not in a week.' There was something here she didn't understand, another undercurrent flowing into the dark, turbulent river that made up her relationship with the Vittorias—and one Vittoria in particular. 'There's another girl, Claire, a friend of mine, and she is very efficient.'

'I was not talking about efficiency,' he said softly, 'but being missed.'

She stared at him for a moment, her eyes wary, before saying, 'Now look, Donato, I told you I'm not into playing games—'

'And *I* am not into the game-playing either,' he bit out savagely, all pretence at coolness gone. 'Have you forgotten Lorenzo, Grace—have you? Because I can assure you the child has not forgotten you! Since my mother's death it is *your* name that is constantly on his lips, *your* love that he is crying for as he refuses all comfort and solace. He was devastated when you left a year ago—'

'Don't you *dare* blame that on me,' she spat angrily. 'You know why I left; you made it impossible for me to stay.'

'You did what you wanted to do.' He had immediately regained control of himself, his voice icy and his face cold and blank. 'You did not think it fitting to discuss your departure with me first; you simply walked away, did you not?'

'You could have followed me,' she said tightly, and it wasn't until she said the words, voicing them aloud for the first time, that she realised she had never expected that he would do anything else but come after her, not in her heart of hearts. But he hadn't. And the days had turned into weeks and the weeks into months and she had slowly died inside, the bitterness of his betrayal on top of everything else she had endured turning her love to ashes.

'To do what?' he asked flatly. 'To begin once again the endless quarrels, the pain, the suffering? I thought you had suffered enough, that you wanted peace.'

'I did; I do.' He had cared so little that he had just let her go. The knowledge beat against her brain, making her voice die and her body go limp. And even now the telegram, the request that she attend Liliana's funeral, had not been sent to her because he wanted to see her, because there was any faint spark of the love they had once shared left in that cold, cold heart. Lorenzo was upset and Donato had thought the boy would be comforted by her presence. It was as simple as that. Oh, she hated him—she did; she loathed, detested, *hated* him. . .

The rest of the journey—along winding roads which passed small villages spangled and pretty in the afternoon sun—was completed without further conversation, the atmosphere in the car thick and heavy and taut with a thousand words best left unsaid.

Grace felt ill with the raw emotion that had taken hold of her and was shocked beyond measure to find that Donato could still affect her so violently. She had hoped, wanted, *needed* to find herself immune to him, to have the assurance that that stage of her life—the Donato stage—was over and done with, that the post-mortems were finally completed. Indifference. . .that was what she had prayed for; she had wanted to be dispassionate and distant, unmoved by hatred and resentment and bitterness, at long last able to put the past to rest.

But now the instigator of all her pain was getting in the way. . . But no, that wasn't quite fair, she corrected herself silently. They had been happy once, before—

Her mind slammed to a halt, recognising its own frailty. She couldn't think of it now; she would break down in front of him and that would be the final humiliation. One minute, one hour, one day at a time; that was what she had told herself all those many, many months ago, and when she managed to keep to that she got through—just.

Nevertheless, as the powerful car ate up the miles and they entered the narrow streets of Sorrento she knew where her first visit had to be; she was being pulled there by something stronger than herself. The scent of lemon groves hung heavy in the air as they climbed into the hills towards Casa Pontina, and when they passed through the large wrought-iron gates into the Vittoria estate she found she was on the edge of her seat.

'Can. . .can we go to the walled garden?' Her voice was the merest whisper but he heard it, his head shooting round and his piercing black eyes fastening on her face.

'I do not think this would be a good idea,' he said quietly. 'You are tired from the journey and Lorenzo is waiting—'

'I don't care.' She glanced at him once before staring fixedly ahead again, but such was the look on her face that he said no more to her, leaning forward and sliding the glass partition aside before giving an order in swift Italian to Antonio.

The Vittoria gardens were huge, bursting with tropical trees and shrubs, cascade upon cascade of sweet-smelling flowers, smooth green lawns, hidden bowers and a fine orchard where orange, apricot, olive, almond, fig and banana trees all lived in harmony, but it was to the tiny, shadow-blotched walled garden that Antonio drove, its ancient walls mellow and sun-soaked and protected by a huge evergreen oak that provided welcome shade in the height of summer.

'Grace?' Donato caught her arm as she went to move past him after leaving the car, turning her to face him. 'Would this not be better tomorrow?' he asked softly, his eyes intent on hers.

'Lorenzo won't mind waiting a few minutes more—'

'I was not thinking of Lorenzo.' His voice had been too harsh and he took a deep breath before he spoke again. 'I was thinking of you,' he said flatly.

But she didn't hear him, her eyes, mind and soul fixed

on the high wooden gate at the top of the long slope that led from the drive, remembering how it had been that day in June, nearly two years ago, when she had been demented with grief.

Donato took her hand as they walked up the stone path and she let her fingers rest in his—she really couldn't find the strength to fight him at that moment—and then he was opening the gate and she stepped into the sheltered confines of the walled garden, her stomach jumping into her throat.

'It looks just the same,' she said softly, and Donato nodded at her side.

'Of course, nothing will be changed here.'

The ancient walls were brilliant in places with trailing purple, red and white bougainvillea, lemon-scented verbenas perfuming the air along with pink begonia and a whole host of other flowers. A small patch of lawn in the middle of the garden had a tinkling fountain at its centre, and several seats were dotted round the small enclosure alongside sweet-smelling shrubs and bushes specially chosen for their fragrance.

It was tranquil, peaceful, a sheltered oasis amidst the bustle of life that surrounded the Vittoria empire, and once Grace had been used to spending lazy hours in the ancient retreat—lazy and exquisitely happy hours.

They walked to the end of the garden now, where a little foot-high wall enclosed a slightly raised small rectangle of ground that was ablaze with tiny flowers, a headstone cut in the shape of a teddy bear bearing the inscription, 'Precious memories of Paolo Donato Vittoria, aged six months, baby son of Donato and Grace. You have taken our hearts with you.'

CHAPTER TWO

'GRACE! Grace!' Lorenzo's welcome was as ecstatic as his face as he caught sight of her, but in the next moment, as she gathered the thin ten-year-old child into her arms, he burst into a storm of weeping, stringy arms tight round her neck.

'Hush, now, hush,' she soothed softly, sitting down on one of the massive stone steps that led up to the studded front door and holding Lorenzo close against her, until the sobs racking the small frame lessened. 'It's all right, darling.' What stupid things we say in moments like these, she thought silently as she nuzzled her chin into the small black head beneath hers. Lorenzo had just lost his beloved mother to whom he had been exceptionally close; of course it wasn't all right. Nothing was all right in his small world.

'I did not know if you would come.' Lorenzo raised dark, tear-smudged eyes to her gentle gaze. 'You have been away so long.'

'I told you Grace would come, did I not?' Donato asked over their heads, his voice soft. 'And now here she is, just as I promised, but she does not want to be drowned before she has set foot inside the house,' he added warningly. 'Benito is waiting to see her too, you know, and he has a few more words in his vocabulary to show her, not all of them good,' he finished darkly.

Lorenzo gave a weak smile and now his voice held a touch of its normal sparkle as he whispered, 'One of the new gardeners taught him some bad words.'

'Did he?' Grace smiled, hugging him close once more before rising. 'And knowing Benito I'm sure he repeats them with great relish?' Benito was Lorenzo's parrot, a huge bird whose big, compact body, strong, rounded wings and short, stout hooked bill were as formidable as

20

his nature. He either loved or hated, there was no halfway house with Benito, and he could use his lethal bill and clawed feet to painful effect on occasion. However, the irascible bird adored his small master, who could do anything with him, and had never suffered so much as a small peck.

Lorenzo took her hand and they moved towards the open front door, and although the small, warm fingers clutching hers were wonderfully comforting, Grace was vitally aware of that tall, dark figure just behind her as they stepped across the threshold of Casa Pontina.

The light, cool hall, with its beautifully polished wooden floor and white walls hung with exquisitely framed paintings, was quiet and still, the air scented with a large bowl of freshly cut flowers, and for a moment Grace couldn't believe that Liliana's tall, gracious figure wouldn't sweep out of the imposing drawing room to greet her, her lined but still beautiful face wreathed in smiles of welcome.

Liliana had lived for her family, loving all three of her children with an intensity that was very Italian, and Grace knew for a fact that Bianca's being adopted had made her even more precious to her mother; that was the way Liliana was. Once Grace had married Donato she had become a second daughter in her mother-in-law's eyes.

Lorenzo pulled her along the hall before she had time to reflect further, past the formal drawing room, ornate dining room and Donato's massive study, and down the two steps that led to the back of the house where the breakfast room, kitchens and two large family rooms were situated. It was through one of the latter, specially designated to Lorenzo and filled with his toys and computer equipment, that they walked, and out onto a small covered patio that overlooked green lawns and trees, and in the far distance the vivid blue of an olympic-size swimming pool.

Benito was sitting on his perch, grumbling to himself as he watched one of the gardeners weeding a patch of salvias some fifty yards away, but at the sound of Grace's voice he showed his pleasure by dancing clumsily and screaming a welcome in his harsh voice, ruffling his brightly coloured plumage and lowering his short neck for her to tickle his head, his bright, beady eyes half closed in delight.

'He remembers me.' Grace was almost reduced to tears by the bird's faithfulness. 'I thought he would have forgotten me by now,' she said thickly, fighting back the weakening emotion as she stroked the beautiful silky feathers.

'You are not easily forgotten.' Donato's voice was low and pitched only for her ears but the hypocrisy hit her as though he had shouted the words, and when she spun round to glare at him hot colour stained her cheeks scarlet. He had been silent for twelve months, not a phone call, a letter, not even a brief postcard, and now he dared to say she was not easily forgotten?

'How is Maria these days?' she asked tightly, as though the question was a natural follow-on to his comment—which to her it was. Maria Fasola: young, beautiful, family friend. . .and Donato's mistress. 'Well, I hope?' she added grimly before he could speak.

'As far as I know.' He looked at her expressionlessly, his eyes veiled and dark. 'Is there any reason why she shouldn't be?'

'None at all.' Her voice was cold and she was about to say more when she noticed Lorenzo's puzzled gaze as he glanced towards them, obviously unsure of what exactly was being said. 'And I need not ask if Benito is well, need I?' she asked the small boy, forcing a playful note into her voice. 'He looks enormous, Lorenzo; I'm sure he has grown several inches since I saw him last.'

'It is because he is fluffing out his feathers, Grace.' The young voice was very earnest; Benito was his pride and joy and could do no wrong. 'He is not fat.'

'Grace! Grace!' The irrepressible bird screeched her name noisily. *'Donato and Grace!'*

'All right—*That is enough!*' Donato waved a finger

at the parrot who stared back at him cheekily, head on
one side as he considered how far he dared go.

'*Enough! Enough!*' he mimicked wickedly. '*Naughty
Benito! Bad bird! Scusi, scusi.*'

Grace saw Donato close his eyes for one infinitesimal
moment and turned away to hide a smile. The autocratic
head of the Vittoria empire might control his family and
those about him with a rod of iron, his power and influence absolute and unquestioned, but in a battle of wills
with Benito the parrot won every time. He was a definite
thorn in Donato's flesh and she couldn't help admiring
the bird's intrepid spirit.

'Come, you must refresh yourself and then Anna will
serve lunch.' Donato took her arm as he spoke, but before
she allowed him to lead her back into the house she
promised Lorenzo she would be back shortly as the small
boy raised an anxious face to hers.

'Grace?' he called after her, his thin voice high. 'You
are not leaving again? You are staying at Casa
Pontina now?'

She felt Donato stiffen at her side and turned slowly,
not knowing how to reply, but then the little white face
in front of her caught at her heartstrings and her well-laid
plan of escape after three days blurred and softened. She
knew how it felt when everything that was normal was
whipped out from under your feet, and Lorenzo was a
sensitive child, very loving and given to deep emotion.
Although he was as close to Donato as the difference in
their ages allowed, he needed the warmth and understanding of a motherly heart at this time, she thought rapidly.

Admittedly there were the female servants—Cecilia,
the elderly cook, and Anna and Gina, the two young
maids—and also the capable tutor Donato employed for
his brother's education, who came to the villa for several
hours each day Monday to Friday, but Lorenzo was not
close to them and, being a Vittoria, had been taught to
maintain a stiff upper lip at all times.

The small boy's love and devotion at the time of
Paolo's death had been an enormous comfort to her, and

now she could do something for him when he needed her most, she reasoned painfully. All she wanted to do was to leave Casa Pontina and the memories of this past life and return to England as fast as she could, but she couldn't abandon Lorenzo now.

In a few weeks, less even, the harsh shock of his mother's death would begin to fade and the mercurial resilience of all children would come into play. This was the important time, the crucial time that might shape his personality for good or ill; she could spare him a few weeks of her life, surely? But could she stand being so close to Donato? She took a deep breath and smiled at the little face watching her so closely. She had no choice, as Donato had known all along.

'I have a home in England now, Lorenzo, but I am going to stay with you until you are feeling better and don't need me any more. Is that all right?' she asked softly, knowing she had done the only thing possible when the small face relaxed and the look of panic and dumb confusion left the big dark eyes.

'*Si.*' He nodded slowly before suddenly running to her, flinging his arms round her middle and hugging her tight, only to leave the room in a mad scamper, head downwards, to hide his tears of relief.

'So. . .' Donato stood with her, looking after the small figure as it disappeared. 'This is not what you envisaged.'

'No, no, it isn't.' His cool, controlled voice grated on her nerve-endings like barbed wire and she raised shadowed eyes to his. He had known what he was doing when he had sent that telegram, she thought bitterly, known her love and respect for his mother would force her to make the journey to Italy in spite of their failed marriage, and that once here she wouldn't turn her back on Lorenzo's plight.

He hadn't bothered about her for months, had continued quite happily with his life here and all it held— an image of Maria's lithe, sleek figure flashed into her mind and she dismissed it abruptly—and then when he needed to use her, and 'use' was the right word, she told herself with acid resentment, had had no compunction about turning her life upside down for a second time.

She saw that the dark gaze had seen into her mind and now Donato shrugged slowly, his voice low. 'I cannot help the love he has for you, Grace; it has always been so.'

And you? You once loved me too, she thought with a pain that shocked her. Before it all went wrong, before the death of our child drove me nearly insane and you into the arms of another woman.

Oh, she shouldn't have come. She turned from him, tears pricking at the back of her eyes with burning ferocity. She should have forgotten Liliana, Lorenzo, all of them, should have stayed in England where the nights were cool and the days humdrum and nothing disturbed her peace of mind.

'Grace, I know this is hard for you—'

'Don't touch me!' As he reached out to her she sprang back with a suddenness that surprised them both, her voice shrill and defensive. 'Don't you dare touch me, Donato. I've said I'll stay for a few weeks until Lorenzo is feeling better but that doesn't give you the right to maul me about.'

'Maul you?' He was utterly outraged, his big, muscular body taut and rigid and his handsome face black with fury. 'I have never mauled a woman in my life,' he said grimly.

'Of course not,' she agreed with icy sarcasm. 'They just fall at your feet all by themselves.' *Like Maria.* She didn't want to feel such anger; she'd thought she had come through the fire of desolation and betrayal and had finally put it behind her, but since the first moment she had seen him again her vulnerability where this man was concerned had hit her as strongly as ever and it frightened her—frightened her more than she could say. 'It amazes you, does it, that any woman could resist your fatal charm?' It was a cheap jibe but she couldn't help it; any defence was better than none.

His eyes continued to hold hers for one more long

moment and then she saw him take a deep pull of air as he shook his head slowly. 'You used to conduct yourself with refinement and charm,' he said tightly. 'What has happened to you that you have become so uncivilised?'

She heard the words as though in a vacuum, the sheer audacity of them failing to register for a few seconds, but when they did her hand shot out to connect with the hard, tanned skin of his face in a resounding slap that actually echoed in the room. 'You can ask me that?' she hissed furiously, her hand drawing back to strike again, but this time his fingers shot out to entrap her wrist in a steel hold that was bruising.

'Yes, I can ask you that,' he rasped, his eyes dangerous and the imprint of her hand beginning to stain the brown skin red. 'I have every right to ask you to explain yourself; I am your husband.'

'Not any more—'

'The courts would disagree with you,' he said harshly. 'You are my wife, Grace, legally and before God. There has been no divorce; the marriage contract still stands.'

'Not in my eyes.' She was panting hard, her slim fairness overshadowed by his dark maleness as he held her fast. 'You might be my husband by contract but that is all, and without love our marriage certificate becomes just a piece of paper.'

'That is a very convenient line of thought but one that is totally without foundation,' he said icily, 'as you well know. Legally—'

'I don't *care* about "legally", Donato,' she ground out slowly, punctuating each word with a significant pause. 'Do you understand that? I don't *care*—about our marriage, you, all of this.'

'No?' Now he drew her closer, his hold on her intimidating rather than restraining. 'But I think this is not altogether the truth, *mia piccola*,' he said with a dangerous softness, 'and I also think you are trying to convince yourself rather than me.'

'Let go of me!' He had both her wrists in his hand now, holding them against the hard-muscled wall of his chest as he fitted her against him, his other hand in the small of her back. She had always been tiny against the hard male breadth and height of him and she knew it was useless to struggle; nevertheless that was exactly what she did do as his dark head lowered to take her lips.

He growled softly, the sound impatient as she postponed the inevitable, and then his mouth covered hers, plundering the sweetness within as he urged her even closer against the hard frame of his body. She fought—for long seconds she fought, even more so when the realisation that his familiar touch and smell were evoking feelings she could well have done without dawned on her consciousness, but eventually she became still, knowing that she couldn't win. She would never win against Donato.

When she had left the Vittoria mansion twelve months ago the same knowledge had had her pale-faced and shaking as Liliana had clung to her, the older woman's normally proud and composed face awash with tears as she had begged her daughter-in-law to wait before asking Donato for the divorce Grace had said was inevitable.

'Why? Why now, Grace?' Liliana had wept, holding the younger woman close to her as they had waited for the taxi Grace had ordered. 'He loves you—I know this, I know it. Please, for my sake, do not be hasty. Give yourself some time apart but do not be hasty.'

But as much as she loved Liliana Grace couldn't tell her what she had learnt only that morning—of Donato's affair with Maria; she had felt too raw, too humiliated at the time. Later she had regretted it, knowing that Donato would have covered his tracks well and that his mother would have been forced to think that she had ended the marriage on a whim, but by then she had made a new life in England and had believed there was always the chance, some time in the future, to put the record straight with Liliana. But 'some time' had never come.

She remembered Liliana's last words to her before the taxi had taken her away. 'This is all a mistake, my dear, and one day you will see it. You have suffered, I know how you have suffered, but Paolo was part of both of you; let your grieving pull you closer together. I shall say to Donato you want time to heal; that is all.'

But it hadn't been her anguish over the death of her child that had driven her from her home and there had been a mistake all right—a great colossal giant of a mistake—and Donato had made it—with Maria. She had crept away that morning a year ago like a small, beaten animal seeking solace in a hole, unable to face another confrontation with Donato and leaving a letter to explain that she had discovered his affair with Maria.

But that had been then. Now she was a year older and a year wiser and more importantly she had survived a year without him; she had become autonomous—something she had thought impossible only months before.

The knowledge brought her senses fully alert, jerking her away from the edge of pleasure his lovemaking had taken her to, and now he let her move from him, his eyes narrowed as she faced him like a small, spitting tabby cat preparing to do battle with a vastly superior wild black panther.

'If you try that again, or anything like it, I'm leaving here regardless of Lorenzo or anyone else. Is that clear?' she spat with all the fury in her heart. 'I came back for Liliana's funeral, and only that, and if your ego can't cope with that truth then I'll get on the next plane home.'

'Oh, I think my ego can survive—just,' he drawled grimly, 'in spite of being pierced through.'

For a strange moment she thought there was an inflexion in his voice that spoke of pain, misery even, but the hard, handsome face was as implacable as always when her eyes searched the sculptured features. Nevertheless the brief second of uncertainty was enough to drain her rage and leave her pale and shaking as she fought for control, her red-gold curls throwing her pallor into even more stark relief.

How could people end up like this? How could they, she asked herself tensely, when they had shared the intimacies of marriage, the birth of a child? Oh, Paolo, Paolo.

'I loved him too, you know.' It was as though she had spoken her thoughts out loud and she started violently as Donato's deep voice cut into her pain, but she could read nothing from his dark face. What was he thinking—really thinking? she asked herself wildly as she stared into the beautiful dark eyes that were like liquid onyx.

Once she had been able to tell, even teasing him on occasion that he could fool everyone else but her with his cold ice-man image, but now? Now she didn't know—didn't *want* to know, she qualified fiercely. If she didn't let him get near her again he couldn't hurt her again. Simple. What wasn't so simple was the seductive need his touch had induced, the sweet, potent ache between her legs and the ripening of her breasts from their contact against his hard chest. But that was physical, just an instinctive response of her body to his as it had recognised the feel and taste of him, and as such it could be controlled. *It could.*

'I know you loved Paolo, Donato.' She didn't try to prevaricate but it was only as she spoke her son's name that she realised she had come a long way from the first devastating weeks of grief. Then the sound of his name had been like a sword piercing her through; now it produced a sad, tender yearning but without the raw, blinding pain. 'We both did; we always will.'

'Then for his sake could we not try to make the next few weeks as easy as possible?' Donato asked quietly. 'You have seen how things are with Lorenzo, you acknowledge he needs you here?' She nodded silently. Yes, she could see the heartbroken little boy needed unconditional love and companionship in the immediate future. 'Bianca has offered to take him into her home for the time being but he does not want that and I agree it would not be good for him. He needs to be in his own home, with things familiar. Benito for one,' he added wryly.

She nodded again, guessing rightly that Bianca had refused to take the parrot; the two had always loathed each other but Benito's dislike took the form of a verbal

assault whenever Bianca was present, and although it
was impossible it always seemed that Benito had planned
exactly what he was going to say for maximum effect,
proving himself a worthy adversary against Bianca's
caustic tongue. Perversely, the parrot adored Romano,
Bianca's husband, screeching with delight whenever
he saw him and nuzzling his hand when Romano
stroked him.

'I shall need to let the surgery know as soon as
possible,' she said stiffly. 'They may need to find a
replacement.'

'Oh, I'm sure they will keep the position open for
you.' His tone was smooth, but with that edge running
underneath which she had recognised before. She ignored
it; her nerves were shot to pieces as it was and she really
couldn't take much more. 'Would you like to telephone
now?' he asked with suspect helpfulness.

'I. . . Yes, I suppose I could.' She stared at him warily.
'Or after lunch; there's no rush.'

'There is also no time like the present; is that not what
you English say?' He smiled, but it didn't reach the
ebony eyes. 'Use the phone in my study; you will not
be interrupted there.'

He took her arm as he spoke, moving her out of the
room and into the lower hall before she could reply, and
although she wanted to speak the touch of his fingers
was burning her through her thin cotton blouse and the
delicious smell of him was sending all lucid thought from
her head.

Why, oh, why did he have to affect her like this? she
asked herself angrily as she trotted along at his side into
the main part of the house. She didn't want it—in the
circumstances nothing could be more humiliating—so
why did her senses go into overdrive at no more than a
lift of those sardonic black eyebrows? It was over,
finished. Her brain knew that, so why wasn't it sending
the message to her hormones? she thought testily.

'Here we are.' He opened the door to his study, standing aside for her to enter first with his normal courtesy

and then following her into the room, shutting the door carefully behind him.

'Would you like me to get the number for you?' he asked silkily, walking across the beautifully furnished room to his large, gleaming walnut desk and picking up the phone before she could demur, his face impassive.

She stared at him, a little taken back without knowing why, but feeling even more certain that there was something running under the cool, controlled façade that was anything but cool and controlled. Following her into the room for what was obviously a private phone call was not Donato's style; his manners were always impeccable, his good breeding absolute.

But perhaps he was merely trying to be helpful? she thought quickly. Especially after their conversation about compromise? 'Thank you.' She gave the number and then took the phone a few moments later when he spoke her name, his voice flat. After settling herself in the chair opposite his desk she hesitated, expecting he would now leave, but instead he strolled lazily to his own chair, seating himself without a word.

She was now positioned so that he was directly facing her across the polished expanse of wood, and he was making no effort to glance at any of the papers on his desk, his eyes tight on her flushed face as she began to speak.

'Hello, Claire, is that you?' she began hesitantly, annoyed to find he was making her nervous. 'It's Grace.'

'Grace?' Claire's voice mirrored her concern and Grace felt warmed by her friend's solicitude. They had only known each other for the last four months, Claire having come to work at the surgery following a long spell in hospital after a severe road accident, but the two of them had immediately hit it off. 'I've been thinking about you all day. How's it going?'

'OK.' She took a deep breath and tried to clear her thoughts, which were gluing together under the rapier-sharp gaze across the desk. 'But I'm going to need to stay in Italy longer than I thought,' she said carefully.

'You are?' Now the anxiety was transparent. 'You're all right, aren't you? I mean, I know it must be terribly difficult with the funeral and Donato and everything, but there's nothing more?'

'Don't worry, Claire, I'm fine.' She would have loved to unburden herself to this friend whom she had only known a short time but to whom she had been able to confide all the pain of the past and fears of the future, but with the dark presence across the desk freezing the air all around her it was most definitely not the time. 'I'll give you a ring once the funeral is over and we can talk properly, but I just thought I ought to let everyone know I shall be away a few weeks.'

'I see. Hang on a mo and I'll put you through to Jim; he left a message that he wanted to speak to you if you rang at any time.' Claire paused before adding, 'Take care, Grace, and don't forget I'm here for you.'

'I won't; thank you, Claire.' As the phone clicked she felt a moment's surprise at Jim asking for her, and then told herself she should have expected it. Jim had joined the team of doctors at the same time that she had returned to England, and the fact that they were two newcomers had produced a certain affinity between them.

Jim was a mild-mannered, patient kind of individual, well suited to his chosen profession, and with her emotions still raw from Donato's betrayal, coming as it had so swiftly after the horror of Paolo's death, she had been grateful for his calm, placid friendship as she had struggled to take up the reins of her new life.

Grace had no immediate relations in England, having been brought up in a children's home from the age of five, when her parents had been killed in a car accident, and all Jim's family were in Scotland, so the two of them had got into the habit of eating together most evenings before they went home to their respective flats.

When Claire had joined the surgery she had accompanied them on occasion, as well as introducing Grace to her parents and friends, but Jim had still maintained a watchful, fatherly attitude towards her which she had thought rather touching considering he was only a few years older than her.

'There is a problem?' She looked up to find the brilliant dark eyes hard on hers.

'No.' She forced a smile. 'I'm just waiting to be put through; I suppose there is someone with him at the moment.'

'Him?' Donato questioned softly.

'Jim Penn.' She flushed as she said the name although she wasn't at all sure why, but there was something at the back of Donato's glittering gaze that was unnerving. 'He had left a message that he wanted to speak to me if I rang.'

'How. . .thoughtful.'

The tone of his voice brought her eyes sharply to his but then Jim's Scottish burr sounded down the line and she forced herself to concentrate on the disembodied voice.

'Grace? What's happening, girl?' he asked loudly, concern in every syllable. She had confided the bare facts of her abrupt arrival back in England to Jim, and when the telegram had arrived he had been dead set against her returning to Italy for the funeral.

'I'm at the Vittoria villa, Jim.' She paused, vitally aware of the big body opposite her which dominated the masculine room. 'And I shan't be returning as quickly as planned so I thought I'd better let you know. I shall be staying in Italy for a few weeks.'

'Why?' The word was harsh and immediate and so unlike Jim's normal mode of speech that she blinked before replying.

'I. . . It's Lorenzo—you know, the little boy?' she said carefully. 'He's very upset and he needs me. It'll be for a while, Jim, so if you and the others think it would be better to find someone else to take my place—'

'There is no question of that.' He sounded very definite and again she blinked, wondering if it was indeed sedate, unemotional Jim at the other end of the phone or if an alien had taken his place while she had been away. 'Your job will be kept open for you as long as it's necessary,' he added in a softer tone.

'That's very good of you.' She wondered if she should ask him to confirm such a statement with the other doctors but decided against it; this new Jim was less approachable than the old one and she wasn't sure how he would take such a request.

'No, it isn't,' he said quickly. 'It's the least we can do. I... We miss you, Grace. The surgery isn't the same without your fairy footsteps bobbing about.'

There was an urgency in his tone that threw her for a moment and her laugh was forced before she said lightly, 'They aren't very fairy-like at the moment; I'm exhausted.'

'How are things?' he asked immediately, and again that throb in the Scottish burr made her flush.

'Everyone is holding up very well.' There was no movement from Donato, not a whisper of sound, but she could almost taste the dark waves flowing from his hard frame. 'I'd better go, Jim; this call must be costing a fortune. I just wanted to let you all know as soon as I could. You couldn't ask Claire to go and see my landlady and explain everything, could you?' she asked carefully. 'I wouldn't like her to think I'm not coming back.'

'Don't worry about that side of things; I'll sort it out,' Jim said quickly. 'I'll go and see her and arrange to let her have a cheque at the end of the month.'

'Oh, there's no need for that; I can send her a cheque from here—' Grace began, but he interrupted her, his voice brisk.

'I'll see to it, Grace; I'd like to. You can settle up with me when you're home.' There was a faint emphasis on the last word and again she flushed; the note of possessiveness in his voice had never been there before and she was sure she wasn't imagining it.

'All right, thank you.' She hesitated a moment and then said, 'Goodbye, then.'

'Goodbye, Grace. Take care, won't you? And...and

don't stand any nonsense,' he said thickly and surprisingly.

'I... No. Right, then, I'd better go...' She was flustered now and it showed, and there was a moment of heavy brittle silence when she replaced the receiver before she could nerve herself to raise her eyes to Donato. The black gaze was waiting for her as she had known it would be.

'Your...friend did not want you to come here?' The words were soft and silky and deadly.

'I beg your pardon?' She had heard him perfectly well but needed time to collect her thoughts after the amazing phone call, during which she had seen a side to Jim she had never seen before.

'He thought you should stay tucked away in safe little England with the rain and the wind and the number ten bus?' Donato asked cuttingly, his voice vitriolic and his face set in pure unyielding granite.

He was jealous. The knowledge brought her eyes wide open for a split second before a surge of anger tightened her lips and raised her small chin. He didn't want her, he had made that patently clear by his silence over the last twelve months, but he didn't want anyone else to have her either! The Vittoria 'ownership' trait in full sail. But to be jealous of Jim—Jim of all people.

And then she remembered the timbre of Jim's voice during the call and found herself flushing with shock. But she had never indicated to Jim, by word or deed, that there was anything more between them than friendship— never; the mere thought of more made her cringe. Jim was like the big brother she'd never had, a steady, dependable rock; if she'd thought for a second he wanted more...

Donato's hard gaze slashed over her hot face and his voice was even softer when he said, 'So? You have not answered my question.' He folded his arms across his broad chest as he spoke.

'Because it's irrelevant,' she said tightly, with bitter resentment.

'I think not.' He smiled, but it was a mere twisting of his lips, his eyes icy. 'I asked you if he advised you not to come. That is a simple enough question, is it not?'

'It's nothing to do with anyone else what I do or don't do,' she said fiercely. 'I make up my own mind; I won't have it made up for me. Is that a simple enough answer?'

'It will do.' He rose so suddenly that she flinched before she could control the gesture. 'Come, I will take you to your room,' he said arrogantly. 'You would like your lunch there?' he continued as he walked to the door. 'In view of your. . .exhaustion?'

The brief pause before the last word was meant to intimidate but she ignored the allusion to her conversation with Jim and smiled coolly, willing herself to sound distant and aloof as she said, 'Thank you, that would be nice.'

Nice? It would be heaven, she thought weakly, preceding Donato out of the room on legs that were distinctly shaky. An hour or two to compose herself before she faced him again seemed like an oasis in the desert right at this moment, and she still had the hurdle of Bianca to overcome as well as the numerous relatives who would be sure to attend the funeral.

When she had first come to Casa Pontina five years ago as a shy and nervous eighteen-year-old she had thought the beautiful old house stretched for miles, and something of that feeling returned now as they walked along the high, elegant hall to the wide, gracious staircase that curved to the upper floor.

Besides the servants' ample quarters, which were situated beyond the kitchens on the ground floor, there were six massive bedrooms in all, complete with *en suite* bathrooms, but when Donato had asked her to marry him two months after their first meeting he had ordered the immediate construction of a new wing to the building. The extension comprised a huge fitted kitchen, high-ceilinged dining room and two reception rooms, and four large bedrooms with bathrooms *en suite* upstairs.

There was no doubt the resulting addition was both

aesthetically pleasing and unashamedly luxurious, but it was the fact that it was exclusively theirs that Donato had revelled in, although she had felt apprehensive and worried that Liliana in particular would feel rebuffed by Donato's move from the main house.

She had been at Casa Pontina one Sunday afternoon just a few weeks before the wedding day when furnishings for her new home were being discussed, and something in her face must have told Romano, who was sitting opposite her at the dining table, how she was feeling.

'Grace?' He had sought her out after tea, which was unusual, taking her to one side and speaking quietly as he had looked down at her from his considerable height. 'You feel uncomfortable about your new home, *si*?'

'Oh, I love it, I do love it,' she said hastily, 'and I can't wait to live there.' She blushed furiously at this point but he pretended not to notice. 'It's just that I don't want Liliana to think we don't want to be with her. It's not that, really.'

'You have told Donato this?' Romano asked gravely.

'Yes, and he said not to worry, that Liliana is happy about the arrangement. The thing is. . .' She hesitated, feeling a bit silly. 'I don't want Donato to think I don't want to live there so I haven't really said anything else.'

'Grace, I have known Liliana all my life, Donato and I have been friends since we were babies, so perhaps you would not think me presumptuous if I spoke to you on this matter?' Romano asked quietly, smiling his rare smile as she shook her head quickly.

'She is very happy that Donato has found you, and even more so that you are everything she would have liked in a daughter-in-law; I know this. She understands her son perfectly and feels it is right and proper that he wishes to be alone with you in his own domain; she even suggested that it might be time for her to move elsewhere. She feels a young married couple need time alone and she is right. This arrangement, therefore, is one that she is in complete harmony with, be assured on that, and also that she cares a great deal for you.'

'Does she?' Grace had no idea how her face had lit up at his words.

'Indeed she does,' Romano said gently. 'In Liliana's eyes she is mostly definitely gaining a daughter rather than losing a son; on this have no doubt.'

'Thank you, Romano.' She had smiled at him as she had spoken and he bowed slightly in acknowledgement, the action very Latin. It wasn't the first time she had wondered how someone like Romano had come to be married to a petulant, attention-seeking woman like Bianca, but as before she dismissed the thought quickly, feeling faintly guilty to be thinking about Donato's sister along those lines.

Romano's words that day were just the reassurance she needed, and she got even closer to Liliana in the next few weeks as a result of them, her mind having been put completely at rest as to what Donato's mother thought of her.

She told Donato what his friend had said when he drove her home that same night, and he nodded in agreement. 'Madre is thrilled you have consented to be my wife; they are all thrilled, but it would not have mattered if I had not had one other person who approved of our match, my love. From the first moment I set eyes on you I knew you would be mine, I *knew* it; nothing could have kept us apart. You are my destiny, as I am yours; I am going to love you as no other woman has ever been loved before.'

And he had—oh, he had. . . Her eyes flickered now as she remembered how wildly passionate he was—something she had only fully appreciated on their wedding night, which had also been her nineteenth birthday, when the restraint he had employed during their courtship had blazed into a raging fire that had both thrilled and frightened her with its intensity.

Nevertheless, in the taking of her virginity he had also taken her to the heights, into an experience where she was pure sensation, liquid and mindless and wholly his. He had been the perfect lover, her ecstasy his ecstasy, her pleasure his first concern, and there had been times when their union had left them both stunned and shaking as they had slowly returned from the world of colour and light and exquisite richness that their lovemaking had taken them into.

But that time was over, dead, finished, slashed into oblivion by his infidelity, and now, as Donato passed the staircase and walked to the heavy carved oak door that led to the separate wing of the house, Grace caught at his arm, her voice taut. 'You don't expect me to stay in Bambina Pontina?' she asked sharply, unconsciously using the nickname they had christened their home with in the early days.

'Of course.' She could feel the muscled strength in his arm beneath her fingers but he was completely still as he glanced down at her small, dainty hand on his body before raising his eyes to her face. 'It is your home,' he said flatly.

'It was.' She could hear the panic in her voice and forced it back as she continued, ' "Was" being the operative word. I've no intention of staying anywhere but in the main house.'

'Grace. . .' Her name was said with deep exasperation and he closed his eyes for a moment before shaking his head slowly. 'Are you going to continue to defy me at every turn? Is this to be my punishment while you remain at Casa Pontina?'

'I'm not defying you. . .well, I am, but not just for the sake of it,' she amended quickly, agitation evident in every line of her slim body and stiffly held head. 'I want to stay in the main house, that's all,' she said firmly, taking a step backwards away from him.

'I see.' He surveyed her for a moment from dark, hooded eyes before continuing, 'And the fact that all your clothes and belongings are as you left them in Bambina Pontina—your books, your records and tapes and so on—this does not mean it makes sense that you should stay there? You have your own sitting room, your own quarters—'

'Donato—'

'And your own bedroom, of course,' he continued smoothly, his face expressionless. 'I moved out of our bedroom shortly after it became apparent you did not intend to return immediately.'

'Shortly after. . .' Her voice trailed away as she stared at him in utter amazement. Her letter had been nothing if not succinct; she couldn't have been more explicit about her non-return.

'So you are quite safe, you understand?' His eyes were mocking now, scornful of her unease. 'I have not yet become so desperate for a woman that I have taken one against her will.'

'I didn't imagine you would do that,' she snapped back quickly, angry that he had sensed her apprehension and wishing she hadn't started the conversation. She couldn't quite explain her reluctance to stay in their old quarters; it wasn't that she imagined he would force himself on her—the mere thought of Donato Vittoria behaving in such an ill-bred way was absurd. It was more. . .more herself she feared.

The thought was shocking and brought her head bolt upright as she faced him, her deep blue eyes dark with confusion and her red-gold hair a blaze of silky fire. She didn't want to feel attracted to him, to acknowledge that dangerous magnetism he exuded as naturally as breathing, not after the way he had betrayed her with Maria, but. . .

But nothing, she told herself with bitter self-contempt at her weakness. He was a man possessed of great charisma and power—from the first time she had met him she had seen women go down before that fascinating and indefinable charm like ninepins—but she wasn't the kind of wife to tolerate liaisons and affairs and what he had done once he could do again. Why was she even thinking like this? she asked herself with very real amazement. There was no question that she would ever put herself in the position where he could betray her again—*none*.

'So. . .' He had been watching the play of emotions over her face with piercing interest although the ebony eyes were hooded and veiled. 'There is no logical reason for you to refuse the privacy and comfort of Bambina Pontina, is there? And it will be reassuring for Lorenzo for life to resume some normality, if only for a short time,' he finished smoothly.

'I. . .'

She stared at him as her mind raced. She didn't want to stay in their old home, not for an hour, a minute, but to admit she feared even the slightest intimacy with him would give that over-sized ego a massive boost. She needed to convince him, and herself, that she was immune to his charm and she would, even if it killed her, she told herself with gritted teeth before nodding tightly.

'I suppose so. I've only brought a few clothes with me so it will be convenient to use the ones I left. I presume they are still in the wardrobe?' she asked quietly, forcing herself to show no reaction to his touch when he took her arm and walked her over to the door leading to the wing.

'Of course.' He sounded almost shocked, she thought grimly. It was clearly all right to cheat on your wife but not to dispose of her belongings. 'Nothing has been touched.'

Her heart began to thump as Donato opened the door and she stepped into the wide, cream-painted hall she had never expected to see again, the beautiful mosaic tiles beneath her feet and the collection of unglazed, lacy-patterned pottery plates on one wall achingly familiar.

'Welcome home, Grace.' His voice was soft and husky and his lips had brushed hers before she could protest, their touch igniting a small flame she strove to hide with harshness.

'I told you not to do that.' She glared at him, her cheeks fiery and her breathing shallow. 'I *told* you.'

'So you did.' He straightened, smiling derisively. 'But I prefer to give orders, not to take them. Besides——' he stopped what was clearly going to be a blazing retort on her part with an uplifted hand '——it is the Italian way to be hospitable.'

'That's not hospitality, it's. . .it's. . .'

'When you find an adequate adjective let me know, but, in the meantime, shall we. . .?' He indicated the beautifully worked wrought-iron staircase with a nod. 'I understand your suitcase is already in your room,' he added smoothly.

'I see.' So he'd had this all worked out from the word go, had he? she thought balefully. 'You're so very sure of yourself, aren't you, Donato?' she said tightly as she shook his hand from her arm. 'So sure you'll always get what you want.'

'Thank you, I like to think so.' It was meant to annoy and it did, unbearably, but she strove not to let it show as she marched across to the staircase with her head held high. He was impossible—this whole *thing* was impossible. She should never have come—Liliana wouldn't, couldn't have expected her to. . . But she would have. The knowledge drummed in her head as she walked carefully up the stairs, painfully conscious of Donato watching her ascent from the hall below, his big, dark frame perfectly still.

Duty, respect, responsibility, sacrifice—Liliana had been of the old school and had lived her whole life by such standards. She would certainly have expected the woman she looked on as a second daughter to attend her formal departure from this world; her non-attendance would have been unthinkable.

White sunlight was slanting through the huge arched windows of the landing as Grace reached the top of the stairs and fairly flew along the polished wooden boards without looking to left or right, almost falling into the room they had designated as the master bedroom and then standing with her back pressed hard against the closed door, her eyes tightly shut.

That dream she had had, the night before the telegram had arrived... Liliana had told her then to come home; she could still hear the urgency in the older woman's voice and see the way her arms had been stretched out towards her. 'He needs you, Grace, more than you could ever imagine. It is only when you come home that the healing can begin. Come home, Grace, come home.'

She had woken from the dream in the middle of the night, shaking and wet with perspiration, her heart pounding and her mouth dry. Had Liliana really called her? she asked herself now, still with her eyes closed. And if so, if the woman she had loved as a mother had reached out from another world for her help, what would be expected of her?

The dream had confused her at the time; she had lain awake the rest of the night until dawn had broken, trying to convince herself it meant nothing, but since her arrival back in Italy she could see it was perhaps Lorenzo Liliana had been calling her for. That, at least, would make some sense, because her first supposition—that Donato's mother had been referring to her eldest son—was too ridiculous to entertain, and she had known it immediately she had brought logic and reason to bear.

She slowly opened her eyes, forcing herself to look round the large, bright, sunlit room that had been her marital bedroom for three years. It was here that Paolo had been conceived after long, lazy hours of sweet love-making just three months after they had been married, hours when she had moaned under the exquisite sensations Donato had produced so effortlessly in her soft flesh, when the sexual feeling that had flowed in and around and through her had been so unbearably wonderful that she had thought she'd die from it...

Was that how he made Maria feel? She forced the name into her consciousness as a talisman against the weakness that was threatening to overwhelm her. Probably, she thought grimly as her eyes began to focus. Very probably. He was an accomplished lover.

And then she saw them, the carefully arranged display

of wild flowers. Michaelmas daisies, blood-red poppies, ragged robin with its delicate pink petals, white and blue forget-me-nots, the deep green leaves and sky-blue petals of germander speedwell, coltsfoot, orange hawkweed, lady's-smock, scarlet pimpernel. . .

'Oh!' Her hand went to her throat as she gasped out loud. Her wedding bouquet, and only Donato knew its significance. She walked across to the flowers slowly and stood looking at them for long moments before tentatively touching the tall spikes of purple loosestrife and pale blue buddleia, the tiny white flowers of shepherd's purse splaying out beneath them.

All through the long years in the children's home she had picked small posies of wild flowers, gathered from the hedgerows and lanes close by, to brighten her windowsill in the dormitory. The delicate beauty of the flowers had been something pure and lovely in the stark, regimented existence within the building where practicality had been the order of the day. They had been a comfort she couldn't explain to anyone, a hope, a promise that life would get better, and when she had nervously tried to explain her feelings to Donato when the expensive hothouse blooms for the wedding were being discussed she hadn't thought he'd listened.

And then, on her wedding day, the most exquisite bouquet had been delivered, tied and threaded through with white silk ribbons and lace, the marvellous array of wild flowers cascading almost to the floor in a declaration to their future.

She had cried then and she knew she was going to cry now. She threw herself onto the scented linen covers of the big double bed, curling into a tight little ball of misery and grief.

How could he? How could he have slept with Maria Fasola, held her, loved her, smiled at her, after all they had meant to each other? Their marriage, the moments they had shared, Paolo's birth, his death—oh. . .oh, his death. . .

Her sobs were wrenched from the depths of her, harsh,

angry, desperate sounds that reached the tall, dark man standing outside the room, freezing his fingers on the handle of the door and turning his face into a mask of stone before he turned savagely, striding away down the passageway with violent steps.

CHAPTER THREE

BY THE time Anna arrived with her lunch tray some fifteen minutes later Grace had washed her face and appeared calm, on the surface at least, but once the small maid had left she gazed down at the *cannelloni ripieni*—pasta rolls with a filling of meat and tomato sauce—on a bed of fresh green salad and sighed wearily.

She had thought she was past the tears, the pain, the sheer rage, but since her first step on Italian soil the past had closed round her like a dark veil. She placed the tray on a small table before lifting the large crystal wineglass and walking across to the full-length windows, opening them and stepping onto the balcony beyond, where she stood in the warm sunshine sipping the cool, fruity red wine. She was still there some twenty minutes later when Donato stepped through the billowing lace curtains.

'You haven't eaten a bite, have you?' He inclined his head backwards towards the bedroom.

'I'm not hungry.' As she spoke she raised her chin at the condemning note in his voice and for a moment blue eyes clashed with coal-black in a battle of wills.

'It will be of no help to anyone if you become ill.'

She didn't know if it was the large glass of rich, potent wine on an empty stomach, the tension of the last day or two since she had received the telegram, the lack of sleep, the memories that had assailed her constantly all day, or just Donato himself in all his arrogance, but suddenly it was all she could do to hold onto her temper.

'No, of course not; that would put a spanner in the works, wouldn't it?' she agreed tightly, her voice lethal. 'My usefulness to the Vittoria empire would be severely affected if I couldn't fulfil my role as companion to Lorenzo—'

'Stop it!' He took a step forward and gripped her arms

with a strength that told her he was angry—very angry. 'That was not what I meant and you know it.'

'I know nothing of the kind, Donato.' She didn't flinch from his wrath, standing straight and still in front of him, her delicate, slender body held taut and her eyes blazing. 'And please let go of me,' she said icily. 'I've told you, I won't be mauled.'

He held her for one moment more, his face working with dark emotion, before turning abruptly aside and moving to stand with his hands resting on the thick stone wall of the balcony, his back bent and his arms outstretched. 'Never, ever have I met such a perverse woman,' he muttered furiously, his head bent downwards.

'I find that hard to believe.' Her voice wasn't as tart as she would have liked it to be, those few seconds of being held close enough to breathe in the delicious smell of him and to feel that big, powerful body having started a reaction in her traitorous limbs she could well have done without.

She watched him take a long, hard pull of air before straightening slowly and turning to face her, his eyes hooded now and his face cold. 'I will order another tray to be sent up and this time you *will* eat,' he said slowly. 'You understand? Dinner will not be until eight and I do not want you feeling faint; you are too thin as it is.'

'Too thin?' She bitterly resented the criticism and glared at him, her blue eyes sparking. He preferred Maria's rounded curves, did he? Full-blown voluptuousness? Well, that was just too bad. 'My weight is perfectly adequate for my height, actually,' she said tightly, 'and I haven't had any complaints so far.'

Why she added that last bit she didn't know but he certainly didn't like it, she thought with great satisfaction as the ebony eyes iced over and his mouth thinned. How dared he? How *dared* he compare her with that woman?

'Is that so?' His voice was silky-soft but with a dangerous edge that warned her she had better say no more. 'And what exactly does that mean, *mia piccola*?' The old endearment was chilling. 'Would you care to elaborate on that enigmatic statement?'

'Not really.' She shrugged, her eyes falling away from his as she tossed her head, annoyed with herself for feeling intimidated.

'Very wise. Your shame does you credit,' he said cuttingly.

The double standard was too much to take and her voice was as sharp as jagged glass as she bit out, 'Now wait just a minute; you've got no right to talk to me like that. We've been separated for a year——'

'You are still my wife,' he interrupted icily. '*Mine*.'

'I want a divorce, Donato.' The words hung in the air for long moments when the two of them were completely still and all nature held its breath, no sound whatsoever breaking the tension.

She shouldn't have told him now, she berated herself miserably; she hadn't intended to broach the matter until well after the funeral, days away, when they were all calmer and emotions weren't at such a painful pitch. This was all wrong——telling him in the heat of the moment when she could hardly think straight——but he had made her so *mad*. . .

'Why?'

'Why?' It was the last thing she had expected him to say, especially in the flat, expressionless tone of voice he had used, and her own voice was high and shrill as she asked again, 'Why? You can ask me that after all that's happened?'

'*Sì*, I can ask you why; I want you to spell it out for me,' he said levelly, 'and I shall know if you are lying.'

'Lying?' This conversation was fast beginning to resemble some sort of weird *Alice Through the Looking-Glass* exchange, she thought wildly. Why should she lie? Weren't the facts bad enough in their own right? 'Why should I lie?' she said, echoing her thoughts. 'You know as well as I do that our marriage is over; there is nothing left between us, Donato.'

'You are asking me this or telling me?' he rasped

scathingly. 'Because if it is the latter then I would remind you that you married me of your own free will, before God and man. You made vows which were for life— *life*; I will permit no divorce to soil the Vittoria line,' he said with a finality that made her see red.

'You will permit no—'

'But if you are *asking* me, Grace—' He interrupted her outrage before she could say more, pulling her roughly into the enclosure of his arms while the words were still on her lips. 'If you are asking me then I will let actions speak louder than words.' He was holding her so securely that she couldn't move as he bent his head but she tried to avoid his mouth nevertheless. 'Don't be silly,' he murmured a second before his mouth closed over hers. 'You cannot escape me and nor do you want to.'

The kiss was not gentle, it was agonised, desperate, and its very hunger was her undoing. If he had used his experience, his considerable finesse in seduction technique, she could have resisted more easily, but the frantic devouring of her mouth was a confession in itself of his need of her and something in her she didn't dare acknowledge rose instantly to meet his desire.

She fought it, for exquisitely painful moments she strove to hide her body's response to his, but then she ceased to think as his lips and tongue searched and explored hers, shooting hot sensation to every nerve and sinew of her small frame. She was on fire, burning up, and she remembered—oh, how she remembered— this feeling. She had been in a desert for so long and it had been so dry, arid. . .

She was aware of the little whimpers sounding deep in her throat as she began to kiss him back but they were out of her control, the heated lips caressing and biting and tasting her own the only reality in a world of blinding colour and sensation, and as he crushed her against him, his arousal surging against her soft flesh, her legs turned liquid.

'Donato. . .' She spoke his name on a little moan but

whether it was a plea or a protest she couldn't have said; his hands had moved to her swollen breasts and their touch had her shuddering and trembling against his hard frame in an agony of sensuality.

'Grace, Grace, it has been so long.' He picked her up in his arms, carrying her through the filmy lace into the bedroom and laying her on the perfumed covers almost reverentially before his hands continued to stroke and caress her. 'You are mine; you will always be mine. . .' The possessiveness in his voice was deep and strong, its triumphant throb cutting through the layers of sexual delight as thoroughly as a knife through warm butter, and it hit her like a deluge of cold water.

'Let me go!' She jerked violently beneath him as she spoke, sliding away from him and off the side of the bed to spring swiftly to her feet. 'I hate you—do you hear me? I hate you,' she panted softly, her eyes wild. All this had been to prove a point, to let her know that he only had to lift his little finger and she would be brought to heel, an obedient Vittoria subject before its master, she thought desperately. There had been no words of remorse, no asking for forgiveness for his betrayal, nothing. A ruler didn't have to explain himself to a subordinate after all. 'Go to. . .to your other women if you want that.' She couldn't say Maria's name; it would stick in her throat.

'Stop this.' His face had been concerned, surprised at first, but at her last words it had frozen over, his eyes narrowing on her flushed cheeks. 'There are no other women.'

'I don't believe you,' she said furiously. 'A leopard can't change its spots and—'

'I said, stop it.' He had been sitting on the bed but as he made a move towards her she stepped back quickly, her hand in front of her and her face twisted with a mixture of fear and outrage.

'I mean it—don't you dare touch me again,' she bit out tightly. 'I told you, there is nothing between us—nothing.'

'Why the hysterics?' His voice was cold now, bitter and angry. 'Is it yourself you are angry at, because you cannot deny you still want me? Or perhaps there is another reason for your somewhat late attempt at virtue? A reason in England?'

'I don't know what you are talking about.' It was true, she didn't, and she didn't care. She just wanted him to leave.

'I hope for your sake this is true,' he said grimly. 'There is an old proverb that says a wise man accuses before he is accused; only a fool waits for the one he has wronged to lay the first charge.' The glittering gaze seemed to bite into her skin.

And then, like a bolt of lightning, what he was insinuating struck her, bringing her mouth wide open and her eyes popping with the sheer audacity of it. He was accusing her of sleeping with someone else——*her*——when all the time, for the last twelve long, painful months and before, he had had a mistress. She stared at him for one more moment before drawing herself up to her full five feet four inches and raising her head proudly, hiding her pain behind veiled eyes.

'If you are suggesting that Jim and I have slept together you are quite wrong,' she said with scathing dignity. 'Jim is a friend and a man of honour; he would no more try to seduce me than fly to the moon.'

'Then he is also a fool.' The dark voice held contempt as well as deep satisfaction. 'Or maybe his ardour is as cold as your British climate?' he added mockingly.

'Jim is the type of man who would be faithful to one woman,' she said with biting directness. 'If that makes him a fool in your eyes it certainly doesn't in mine. He also wouldn't dream of making a move on a married woman, whatever his personal feelings were. Of course I don't expect you to understand either of those attributes,' she finished with trembling resentment.

'No, of course you don't,' he agreed with a silky coolness that told her remark had hit home. 'I am the philanderer, the heartless beast——is that it? And this Jim is as pure as the driven snow? But it is *me* you respond to, *me* who can make you come alive in a way no other man can—'

'Oh, you'd love to believe that, wouldn't you?' she interrupted cuttingly. 'The great Vittoria ego has to have its daily nourishment.' Her words were a defence against the blinding anguish that was threatening to reveal itself to those piercingly intent eyes; inside she was screaming and calling herself every kind of fool for coming back to this house.

The cords to hold her to his will were already snaking around her and they were all powerful in their different ways; Lorenzo's need of her, her love for Liliana, which was prompting her to do what she knew the other woman would have wanted, the weakening knowledge that she had felt closer to Paolo earlier today when she had been in the walled garden than at any other time in the last few months. And there was something else. . .something she dared not even try to examine or understand, just a great burning ache inside of her that was eating her up.

'Why the antagonism, Grace?' He didn't move a muscle but as he spoke, his voice soft and strangely flat, she felt as though he had reached out and touched her. 'I had hoped the time apart would let you see things as they are, that you would at least be prepared to talk about the future, about us.'

'There is no us,' she said quickly. 'There isn't.'

'Are you trying to convince me or yourself?' he asked softly. 'You're mine; you've always been mine since the day you were born. There is no escape from your destiny. This Jim—' he flicked a scornful hand Latin-style '—he is the mist that evaporates before the sun on a summer morning—easily forgotten. If I had not known this I would have fetched you back long ago—either that or there would have been murder done,' he finished darkly.

'Fetched me back?' The pain and anguish were consumed by sheer rage. 'I'm a *person*, Donato; I have a mind of my own. I'm not a servant or a chattel or—'

'I know this.' There was something in his voice she

couldn't quite put a name to. 'I have always known it. I have merely been waiting until you discovered it too,' he said with a disturbing intentness.

'Until I discovered it?' She stared at him, unsure of what was being said. 'I didn't have to discover it.'

'*Sì*, you did,' he said steadily. 'Look into your heart, Grace; have the courage to search your feelings.'

'I don't need to search my feelings,' she shot back quickly, 'I know exactly what I think.' He had the nerve to stand there and explain away the lack of contact over the last year by saying he'd been waiting for her to *discover* herself? she asked herself silently with a touch of hysteria. Well, she knew what he had been discovering, and with whom, and if he thought she was still the gullible, innocent girl he had married who would swallow such a story he was wrong.

Suddenly the whole catastrophic mess overwhelmed her, taking away the rage and resentment and leaving a sad weariness in its wake.

'Donato, post-mortems at this late stage won't do either of us any good,' she said flatly, turning away from him to look towards the lace curtain billowing gently in the warm breeze. 'Perhaps if Paolo hadn't died, if things hadn't started to go wrong, we could have made a go of it, but now. . .now it's all too late. I know I shut you out, that I made mistakes too, but the past is the past; neither of us can alter what's happened.'

'The past is there to learn from—'

'No!' She interrupted his soft voice with a violent gesture of repudiation as she swung to face him again. He was suggesting she should accept his infidelity? Forgive him and forget it and carry on as before? But she had told him in the letter, in the desperate outpouring of her heart, that that was the one thing she could never come to terms with and the past year had not changed her mind. Oh, she knew there were women who could rise above such things for the men they loved, even turn a blind eye if the same thing happened again, but she just wasn't made like that and she knew it. 'I want a divorce and that's that,' she said painfully.

'The hell it is.' The soft tone hadn't altered, which made the quiet words all the more threatening.

'Are you refusing to be reasonable?' she asked stiffly, forcing herself to stare straight at the hard, cold face that had turned to granite.

'Dead right.' His eyes were narrowed and keen on her white face. 'I have never pretended to be a reasonable man and I see no reason to start now. We are married; there will be no divorce. Now. . .' he turned away from her even as he spoke and walked with the lazy animal grace she remembered so well to the bedroom door. 'I will order another tray to be brought to you immediately and then you will sleep. You are overwrought and not thinking clearly.'

'I. . .' His sheer arrogance took her breath away and as she spluttered to find the words to blast an inroad into the colossal self-esteem he turned, his face blank and expressionless.

'You are pleased with the flowers?' he asked flatly.

'The. . .? Oh, yes—yes, thank you.' He had completely thrown her and it showed. 'But—'

'Till tonight, Grace.' And then he was gone, leaving her shaking with rage and something else—something she didn't care to define but which made her heart pound and her mouth dry.

He was just the same, worse if anything, she thought angrily as she began to pace the floor, her hands clenched into fists at her sides. Egotistical, overbearing, sweeping everyone and everything aside so that the Vittoria will had predominance. She sank down onto the quilted easy chair at the side of the window as her trembling legs threatened to give way, her eyes falling on the vast display of flowers that were perfuming the room with an English summer, their colours merging together in soft harmony.

It must have cost him a fortune to organise and get the flowers here, she thought bewilderedly. Half of them were native to England. Why had he made such a gesture?

Her brow wrinkled and she felt the headache she had claimed earlier become a reality. Did he still care for her, in spite of his liaison with Maria? Were the flowers a declaration, a promise that the future would be better? Or were they merely a psychological weapon with which to get into her mind, to dominate and subjugate her to his authority? He had an intimidating intelligence, she knew that only too well, and also a discerning and frighteningly powerful ability to understand friend and foe, and she really wasn't sure which category he placed her in.

'Oh, what does it matter anyway?' she asked herself with a touch of self-contempt at her thoughts. Whatever his motive the past was history, unchangeable, and they were locked into a parting of the ways as inexorably as winter followed autumn. Whether he accepted it or not the Vittoria name *would* have to endure the smear of a divorce and she *would* leave this place, once Lorenzo was sufficiently at peace with the new order of things to take her leaving in his stride.

She would never, ever become a real wife to Donato again; she would rather die first, she told herself fiercely, remaining locked in thought until the maid's timid knock brought her to the door where she took the tray with a word of thanks.

Grace ate every mouthful of the pasta and salad this time, washing it down with another large glass of wine before lying down on the fresh linen covers of the bed and falling immediately into a deep, dreamless sleep that spoke of her utter exhaustion.

She awoke to the shadows of evening stretching into the room, and lay for some minutes in numb inertia, watching tiny particles of dust as they spun and dived in a shaft of dying golden sunlight. She didn't want to think or feel, she acknowledged drowsily as the sound of voices in the gardens beyond the open window intruded into her stupor. She had learnt in the days and weeks following Paolo's death that the only way to get through, to stop herself going crazy, was to close off her mind and enter a vacuum where nothing could touch or reach her. It had worked mostly, enabling her to drag herself through the other times when her grief had threatened to destroy her sanity.

Paolo. . . Her heart twisted as she pictured the sweet little face with its mop of black curls but she was thankful she could see her precious baby that way now; for a long time the image of a still, stiff little shape half-hidden under the thin cotton sheet had haunted her days and nights.

They had been so happy that morning, she mused pensively, awaking late after a night filled with love-making and dreams for the future. 'Bring Paolo back with you and feed him here,' Donato had suggested when she had leapt out of bed on discovering how late it was. 'I like to see my wife feeding my son and heir; it gives me a feeling of authority,' he'd drawled as she had scampered from their room.

'As if you need that!' She had turned at the door to give him a wide smile, her voice mocking. It had been the last time she'd smiled for months, she reflected painfully.

Her screams had brought Donato racing into Paolo's nursery and it had been he who had lifted the tiny body from the cot, shouting at her to ring for a doctor before he had tried mouth-to-mouth resuscitation on his baby son. But it had been too late, far, far too late. They had learnt later that Paolo had been dead for hours—hours of lying still and alone in his solitary little cot.

And she hadn't known. The anguish filled her again and she fought against its pain. What kind of mother was she that she hadn't known Paolo needed her, that he'd stopped breathing? *Cot death.* The two words she'd read about so often with a sad shake of her head for the parents involved had become a terrifying and macabre reality— a reality that was unbelievable, unimaginable.

'Has he been unwell at all? A fever—something like that?' the doctor had asked them much later. He was an old friend of the family and he had clearly been shaken by the tragedy as he had sat facing them in the drawing room, Donato one side of her and Liliana on the other, their hands clasping her ice-cold fingers.

'He's teething.' Her mind had refused to accept Paolo was gone and she had used the present tense. 'He's been a bit snuffly, but he hasn't been miserable or unwell.'

'I see.' The doctor had nodded gravely. 'Well, in cases like this a slight cold is often noticed the day before.'

But she hadn't noticed, had she? She had stared at the doctor, her head spinning. She hadn't noticed and now her child was dead; he had died while she and Donato had laughed and talked and made love. The screaming in her head had filled her mouth and she hadn't felt the injection the doctor had given her. When she had awoken from the drugged sleep she had started screaming again and this time he had knocked her out for twenty-four hours, after which she awoke to a world that had irrevocably changed, a world that was all grey, with no colour at all.

They had all told her it wasn't her fault and Donato—the pain intensified as she remembered and she sat up abruptly—Donato had sat with her for days and nights, talking to her, crying with her, holding her tight when she had thought she was going mad.

She had slowly struggled back to some semblance of normality—on the surface at least—but almost without realising it had gone deeper and deeper into herself, punishing herself with isolation as she had cut herself off from all sympathy and help.

Had she driven Donato into Maria's arms? It was a thought that wasn't new to her, and now she rose from the bed and stripped off her crumpled clothes quickly, walking into the magnificent *en suite* bathroom and standing under the warm, silky water in the shower cubicle for long minutes.

But Bianca had said the affair had started months before she had found out, at Grace's twenty-first birthday party when Paolo had only been gone a short while. She had been suspicious for a long time before the morning she had cornered Bianca on one of her visits to her mother, she remembered painfully, and demanded that the Italian girl explain the latest in the many sly hints and subtle innuendos she had been dropping.

It might have been better if she had asked Donato directly but she hadn't been able to bring herself to do that, the gnawing doubt and jealousy prompted by Bianca finding a release in provoking him into one argument after another as she had striven to make him prove he still loved her, testing him over and over again for some reassurance.

'Donato and Maria?' Bianca, her slanted black eyes cold with dislike, had faced her in the hall of their wing after Grace had pulled her through the connecting door. 'I only said they were having lunch together, did I not?' she'd said haughtily.

'No, you said they were having lunch together *again*,' Grace stated flatly, 'and this isn't the first time you've suggested something more than friendship between them. If you're not prepared to tell me what you know I shall ask your mother.'

'Madre knows nothing about it.' The reply was swift and sharp. 'You say nothing—nothing to her. She has been so upset by all that has happened. I forbid you to speak to her and upset her further.'

'You think I haven't been upset?' Grace said painfully. Donato's sister had been sweetness itself when others were present but the cool hostility she had always shown her when they were alone hadn't wavered in spite of Paolo's death.

'You?' Bianca took a step towards her, her body slightly bent and her neck stretched. 'You English do not feel as we feel; you do not have the fire in your hearts. If Paolo had been mine I would still be inconsolable— but then I would have taken more care of him in the first place—'

The crack of Grace's hand across her face caused Bianca to stagger slightly, but then she righted herself, her eyes venomous. 'You ask me if Donato and Maria are together?' she asked softly, her voice of a tone that caused the hairs on the back of Grace's neck to prickle. 'But why ask me when you already know the truth? Maria is beautiful, and she has always loved Donato; she should have been his wife, not you.

'You remember your party, when you retired early? That was when it began. He was late joining you that night, wasn't he? Because he had been with a woman— a real woman, not a pale reflection of one,' she added spitefully, clearly enjoying the moment.

'I don't believe you.' Grace actually took a step backwards, as though from something evil. 'Donato wouldn't—'

'Has he not been different from that night?' Bianca hissed softly, seeing the confirmation of her words in Grace's face and nodding slowly. 'You see? He has had enough of your pale English body, your frigidity, your cold and unwelcoming bed. His love for you has gone, like Paolo; there is nothing here for you any more.'

Bianca started to say more, her voice low and vitriolic as her words polluted the very air, but Grace pushed her out of her home before sinking down against the closed door and crying until there were no more tears left. And then she phoned the airport, and then a taxi, packing the bare minimum in one suitcase before sitting down and writing Donato a letter telling him what she had learnt from Bianca.

Liliana was alone when she went to say goodbye just before the taxi was due, and she was grateful for that, knowing she was incapable of seeing Bianca again that day without doing something she'd regret.

Grace came out of her thoughts to the realisation that the water had cooled and she was cold. 'It's the past; it's all in the past,' she told herself shakily as she walked through to the bedroom swathed in a huge fluffy bathsheet, her gaze drawn in spite of herself to the spot on the bed where she had left Donato's letter. 'And he doesn't still love me,' she murmured softly, turning to look at the flowers which were suddenly a mockery. 'He doesn't want a scandal, he's made that plain, and Lorenzo needs me. That's all it is.'

She knew it, she'd always known it, so why did the knowledge pierce her through? she asked herself helplessly. She was over him—she *was*; it was just the memories this place evoked that had upset her, that was all.

The knock at the door didn't register on her consciousness until it was too late; by then Donato was already stepping into the room, only to stop at the sight of her, her damp curls clustered round her head like a silky red-gold halo and the bath-sheet draped round her tiny frame. 'I did knock.' He was staring at her mouth, which she had always considered too generous and which he had termed passionate, and the look in his eyes made her bones melt before she pulled herself together.

'I didn't hear you,' she managed with some degree of coherence. 'I. . .I've had a shower,' she added weakly.

'A shower?' He spoke as if the words were incomprehensible before visibly taking a deep breath and continuing in the deep, husky tone she had heard so often in the past, 'There was a time when we used to shower together; do you remember? I would soap you and you would soap me—'

'Donato—'

'And you would make me clean so nicely, *mia piccola*.' His eyes were dark and glittering and she knew by their satisfied expression that she was as red as she felt, but the pictures his words had conjured up in her mind were so real she couldn't help it. He had a magnificent body, she thought silently as she let her long lashes cloak her eyes. Wide, muscled shoulders and a strong chest covered with dark, curling body hair that tapered to a line over his flat stomach and down into—

'What do you want?' She shut off her thoughts with a snap, her voice shaking. She wouldn't be drawn into playing his games.

'Right at this moment?' he asked wickedly, the magnetism that was an essential part of his attraction reaching out and making her knees weak. 'Well. . .'

'I mean, what did you come here for?' Panic made her voice high and she took a silent pull of air before continuing, 'I thought dinner was at eight.'

'It is,' he agreed laconically. 'I just came to say I forgot to mention that Bianca and Romano will also be here.' He spoke his sister's name without the slightest change of tone and Grace stared at him for a moment, her thoughts racing. It had been Bianca who had first alerted her to his affair with Maria, although of course Donato didn't know that; but the letter had stated that Bianca had told her everything. She hadn't felt the slightest compunction at the time about telling Donato who had revealed his indiscretion, and she didn't now, but she had often wondered about how he had viewed his sister's veracity.

Well, she had her answer now, she thought flatly. He didn't care. Bianca was still the spoilt little baby sister who could do no wrong and she was. . . What was she? she asked herself bitterly. His possession, his property, something he owned that had been resurrected after a year of lying idle because it could be useful to him again? Oh, she was a fool—the biggest fool in the world.

'OK, you've told me now.' It didn't take any effort to make her voice cold and stiff; her thoughts had chilled her through. 'And I'd like to get dressed now; if you don't mind?'

'Certainly.' He waved a lazy hand towards the large walk-in wardrobe that took up all of the far wall. 'Be my guest—or should that be my wife?' he added softly as he proceeded to sit himself down in a chair with easy grace, crossing one knee over the other and clasping his hands at the back of his head before leaning back to watch her intently with dark, narrowed eyes.

'I prefer to dress alone,' she snapped tightly after one angry glare which he ignored with regal indifference, 'without an audience, and I thought I had made my position here clear?'

'Crystal-clear.' His face straightened and hardened but he remained sitting. 'However, I thought it might be opportune to fill you in on the funeral arrangements before dinner, when Lorenzo will be with us—*sì*? It will be hard enough on him as it is.'

'Oh. Oh, yes.' She flushed painfully. 'I. . .I'm sorry.'

He acknowledged her apology with an impatient wave of his hand before he began to speak, detailing the schedule in a cool, clipped voice before rising abruptly as he finished. 'You will take care of Lorenzo, Grace?' he asked tersely. 'The boy will find the day hard but it will help that you are there.'

'You're not making him come to the funeral?' She stared at him, aghast. 'But that's cruel. Why can't he stay here?'

'He could stay here; in fact that was exactly what I wanted him to do,' Donato said tersely, his anger at her criticism evident in the blackness of his face. 'However, he insisted he wanted to come and in this matter he is old enough to make up his own mind; he is not a baby when all is said and done.'

'I disagree.' Her guilt in jumping to the wrong assumption about Lorenzo's presence at the funeral made her voice defensive and sharp. 'He's just a child—you know he is.'

'He is ten years old, nearly eleven, and he is a Vittoria,' Donato stated darkly. 'That means in spite of his sensitivity he has a mind of his own and a will of iron. Now, I could oppose him, order him to stay behind, but I do not think that would be the best thing for Lorenzo. He has thought it out and he wants to come; the matter is settled.'

'I don't understand you.' She glared at him, unaware of how very tiny and delicate she appeared to the big, dark man in front of her, her pale, creamy skin almost translucent in the evening light and her eyes dark pools of glowing sapphire against the snowy whiteness of the big towel clutched to her body.

'That is abundantly obvious,' he said crisply, 'but

something I shall not lose too much sleep over. I will not be persuaded from my decision by black looks and tantrums, Grace. Have I made myself clear? Have I?' he pressed when she remained silent.

'Crystal-clear.' She repeated his earlier words with a biting contempt that made his eyes narrow before he moved to step in front of her, raising her chin with a thoughtful finger.

'So much rage and antagonism,' he said slowly, 'for such a tiny little thing. What has happened to you, Grace? You are not the girl I married.'

'No, I'm not.' The agreement was instant and cutting. 'I've grown up, Donato. I too have a mind of my own and a will of iron; it is possible in people other than Vittorias, you know.'

'But you are a Vittoria, *mia piccola*,' he said with quiet grimness, his eyes hard and glittering. 'And perhaps it is time you were reminded of the fact.'

She felt hot tension and fear snake down her limbs as his hand moved to the nape of her neck, stroking the soft, silky skin with an assurance that made her tremble. 'Don't!' She jerked her head away only to wince in pain as his fingers tangled in the riotous, burnished curls. 'Don't,' she said again, her voice frantic.

'Why?' He pulled her head back slightly, his eyes devouring her mouth in a way that made her ache with hidden excitement. 'It is legal, Grace, or did you not know?' he asked arrogantly. 'You bear my name; you are mine.'

'Only if I choose to be.' She kept her body straight and stiff and her voice flat as she silently called on the will she had proclaimed a few moments earlier to fight the intimidating magnetism that was reaching out to ensnare her. *She wanted him.* Physically she wanted him very much, and although it was more than a little galling to acknowledge the hunger that was burning her up it was there. 'And I've told you that I don't, haven't I?'

'I do not believe you.' The black eyes were devilish. 'We both know the fire that has always burnt between

us; if I start to make love to you it will consume us both.
I would not have to force you.' He pulled her slightly
closer, his voice hypnotic.

'Perhaps not.' She saw the dark gaze smoulder with
satisfaction and continued hastily, 'But afterwards everything would be the same; I still wouldn't be yours, not
in here where it counts.' She touched the towel across
her heart as she spoke, praying the trembling deep in her
body wouldn't make itself known to those merciless eyes.
'You wouldn't be getting me, Donato, not the real me,
just a brief physical satisfaction, an act of lust, and I
would hate you afterwards.'

'Perhaps I do not care,' he ground out harshly, shaking
her slightly as he looked down at her. 'Perhaps after
twelve months—*twelve months*—I do not care what is
in your mind. Have you thought of that? We are married,
you are my *wife* and I want you; it is really as simple as
that, is it not?'

'Is it?' She kept perfectly still, knowing one wrong
move could take the situation out of control. 'In spite of
everything that has happened I don't believe you mean
that; it would make you little better than an animal and
the Vittoria name worthless.'

'And you are concerned about the honour of the
Vittoria name?' he asked with mocking bitterness.

'Yes.' She stared back at him steadily. 'My son bore
that name.'

He continued to look down at her for one more
moment, one taut and agonising moment, before thrusting
her aside so roughly that she almost fell, his face working
with a thousand emotions.

'Damn you, Grace.' His face was black with rage, his
accent very pronounced as he strode angrily across the
room. 'What the hell have you turned me into?' He spun
round in the doorway with a violence that was tangible,
surveying her bitterly with hard, blazing eyes before
banging the door so savagely that the whole room shuddered and whimpered before sinking into an unearthly
silence.

CHAPTER FOUR

GRACE stood perfectly motionless for a full minute after Donato had left, willing back the tears with clenched teeth and closed eyes as she clutched the towel to her. Once the thudding of her heart and cramped stomach muscles had relaxed a little she took a long, hard gasp of air, opening her eyes and staring blindly ahead.

So he still wanted her physically, she thought painfully, but so what? That was nothing; men could perform the act without it meaning a thing to them beyond the easing of their body, and she had better remember that. She happened to be here now, convenient and available in his eyes, but it was the months of silence that spoke volumes. He hadn't come after her, hadn't phoned or even written a letter to explain or excuse himself; he just hadn't considered it worth the bother. She blinked furiously, angry that it still mattered so much.

She walked over to the beautiful antique full-length mirror in one corner of the room, surveying her flushed face and trembling lips with something akin to despair before her gaze dropped to her left hand on which her engagement ring and wedding band gleamed brightly. She had thought about taking them off many times in the last twelve months but somehow...somehow it had seemed immoral, deceitful, although she couldn't explain why, even to herself. Once she was divorced it would be different.

The glittering diamonds in her star-shaped engagement ring mocked her, bringing memories of the evening Donato had presented it to her. 'You are my sun, moon and stars,' he had said softly, 'my life, my reason for living. I knew it from the first moment I saw you, so tiny and perfect and unforgettable. You are mine, Grace, as I am yours; this will always be so.'

And just five years later it was over. She raised her head as her mouth hardened, dropping the towel and standing naked before the glass as she examined the slender lines of her body. There was nothing to suggest she had ever had a child; her silky skin was untouched by stretch marks and all the other drawbacks pregnancy could involve, her small, high breasts were still as pert and full as ever, but she *had* given birth to a son, with Donato at her side urging her on.

She closed her eyes tightly for a moment, a stab of pain piercing her through. They had wept with joy when Paolo was born and agonised with bitter tears of grief when he had been taken from them so abruptly, and then within months Donato had been sleeping with someone else. That—*that*—was this grand, all-consuming love he had professed for her, and at the bottom of her heart she had known all along the fairy-tale would end.

She bent and retrieved the towel without looking at herself again, wrapping it round her before walking over to the wardrobe and choosing a light, formal dress for dinner. Once dressed she applied a smoky grey eyeshadow to her eyelids, which darkened her eyes to midnight-blue, and after a cursory touch of mascara on her long, thick lashes put her make-up bag away. She wasn't going to titivate, she told herself tightly, and she wasn't in competition with anyone. Nevertheless, the image of a tall, slim Italian girl with long black hair and golden-brown eyes was at the forefront of her mind as she left her room a little later.

Maria Fasola, a close friend of Bianca's, had never made any secret of her adoration for Donato; Grace had even teased him about it in the early days of their marriage. She felt her stomach turn over at the thought of them together and then put the picture out of her mind. She was going to spend some time with Lorenzo before dinner and concentrate on him and him alone; his older brother was of no concern to her now—*he wasn't*.

She didn't investigate the rooms downstairs; she didn't want them to be the same and yet the idea of them being any different was painful, and it was the same mixed set of emotions that kept her from visiting the nursery. Instead she walked down the staircase and straight through the hall into the main house, her heart beating as fiercely as though she had been running. This had been her first real home, and it still *felt* like home, but of necessity she had to distance herself from it now, close her mind to its pull on her heartstrings. There was no going back.

'Grace! Grace!' Lorenzo's welcome was almost as fervent as earlier that day, and the small boy ran to her, hugging her round her middle for long seconds as she entered his sitting room. 'I am so glad you have come, Grace.' The big, beautiful dark eyes, so like Donato's, were touchingly serious as Lorenzo drew away to look up into her face. 'I prayed that you would, every night without fail,' he said earnestly.

'Did you?' Grace forced herself to smile at the grave little figure when what she really wanted to do was burst into tears and hug him close. But that wouldn't help Lorenzo and it certainly wouldn't help her, common sense told her firmly. There had already been tears, and there would be more in the future as he struggled to come to terms with the loss of his mother, but her job was to try and direct his mind away from the tragedy as much as she could. 'Then maybe that was why I felt I had to come back for a while.'

'I think so. If you want something badly you have to make it happen,' Lorenzo stated solemnly, and this time she had to suppress a real smile as she looked down at him. That incredible Vittoria arrogance! Lorenzo had it, even at the tender age of ten, and in spite of his sensitive and gentle nature he still possessed the deep-rooted and unshakeable conviction that what he wanted would come about simply *because* he wanted it.

It was more than the normal trusting innocence most children had; it was. . .it was pure Vittoria, she told herself shakily, but she was immensely glad of that inner confidence right now. Lorenzo needed all the help it could give him. 'Please stay,' the small boy added quietly. 'For ever, I mean.'

'*Grace! Grace! Donato and Grace. Poor Benito. Poor Bird. Ciao, Ciao.*' Benito had decided he had been out of the limelight too long and now danced on his perch, his harsh voice raucous in the poignant atmosphere and his beady eyes fixed on Grace.

'Hello, yourself.' As Lorenzo turned round with a high giggle of delight she blessed the parrot for his timing. 'And what's with this "poor bird" anyway?' she continued as she walked across to scratch the parrot's head. 'I've never known such a fortunate bird as you, Benito. Plenty of food, a beautiful home and a master who loves you; what more could any parrot want?'

'*Frutta! Frutta!*' The bird sang out its favourite food and Grace reflected, as she had done many times in the past, that the parrot was more human than animal.

The three of them spent a therapeutic hour together, in which Grace was sure Benito conspired with her to take Lorenzo's mind off the events of the next day, and so it was with a very real sense of shock that she heard that purring female voice from the past speak from the doorway some time later, just as she and Lorenzo were laughing at the parrot's ridiculous antics.

'Grace.' Bianca's voice was barbed wire coated with honey. 'Donato told us you have come for the funeral. You must be desolate, *si*?' The slanted dark eyes raked their smiling faces, the message perfectly clear. They should be sad, sombre. . .

'It was Benito—he made us laugh; he—'

Grace interrupted Lorenzo's agitated explanation with a calm voice and a soothing hand as she drew the child to her, her eyes fixed on the beautiful cat-like face in front of her. 'Hello, Bianca.' She nodded to Romano, who was standing just behind his wife with Donato, before turning to Bianca again. 'Yes, I am devastated by the death of your mother, as anyone who was fortunate enough to know her would be. She was the mother I never had,' she added simply, the throb of pain in her voice too moving to doubt.

Lorenzo had immediately picked up on what Bianca was really saying, she thought silently as the Italian woman gave her a stiff nod in reply, just as he had done ever since she had first joined the family. How come a child of ten could be so perceptive and the two men behind her so dumb? she asked herself tightly, furious at their lack of insight. She didn't mind Bianca's criticism of herself, but to suggest Lorenzo shouldn't experience a momentary lifting of his spirit was too cruel for words. His sister knew how devoted the child had been to Liliana; didn't Bianca have any sensitivity at all?

'How are you, Grace?' Romano drew her gaze back to him, his dark, good-looking face smiling and his voice pleasant. She liked Romano, she always had, but he was very much like Donato inasmuch as the outward shell revealed very little of the man within. 'I am very pleased to see you again although I wish the circumstances could have been different.'

'I'm well, thank you.' She would have said more but Bianca had sauntered past her, walking over to Benito's perch on the patio where she surveyed the parrot with transparent dislike.

'It is not healthy that this animal lives here,' Bianca said loudly, her almond-shaped eyes cold. 'Look at the mess it makes. It is not nice; it is dirty.'

'He is not dirty.' Lorenzo sprang to his pet's defence, his small face scarlet with indignation. 'He is perfectly clean.'

'The parrot is Lorenzo's companion.' Donato's voice was deep and expressionless as he spoke from the doorway. 'As well you know, Bianca. And he is normally well behaved.'

Bianca's finely shaped eyebrows lifted in disbelief, but even as she opened her mouth to refute her brother's statement Benito responded to the taut atmosphere with a wicked cackle of amusement. *'Bianca. Oh, Bianca,'* the parrot intoned miserably, his round eyes dancing with

delight in strict contrast to his voice. 'Bianca phew. . .'
The bird gave a first-class imitation of the sound of
someone smelling something obnoxious before dancing
to one end of his perch as Bianca glared at him, her face
poisonous.

'Did you hear that?' She swung round to face the
others, her temper further incensed by the smiles they
couldn't hide. 'It insulted me; the creature insulted me.
It is evil.'

'Oh-h-h. . .Bianca.' Benito was thoroughly enjoying
himself now and it showed. There followed a remark in
Italian that brought Lorenzo's hand tight across his mouth
as he looked across at his brother, his glance wide and
apprehensive.

'That gardener.' Donato shut his eyes for a moment
but Grace was sure she saw his mouth twitch before he
turned to Romano, who was looking at him with a startled
expression on his face. 'The new gardener thought it
entertaining to teach Benito some. . .colourful phrases,'
he explained, deadpan. 'Unfortunately we are not able
to persuade the parrot to forget them.'

'It is disgraceful.' Bianca was seething, her cheeks
scarlet. 'Utterly disgraceful. This animal is not a fit pet
for Lorenzo; it must go. Madre would have insisted
upon it.'

'I think you have said more than enough,' Romano inter-
vened swiftly, his voice bland and calm but his eyes
narrowed as he glanced across at his wife. Bianca obviously intended to say more but as her eyes met those of her
husband Grace saw her stiffen for an infinitesimal moment
before she shrugged sulkily, her cheeks flaming and her
eyes flashing as she brushed past Grace and Lorenzo.

'Donato, Benito did not know what he was saying,'
Lorenzo began tearfully. 'It is not his fault—'

'Do not distress yourself.' Donato's voice was soft but
his expression was wry as he glanced at the object of
their conversation, who stared back at him cheekily, head
on one side and round, bright eyes satisfied. Grace knew
exactly what Donato was thinking and she had to agree

with him; somehow she was sure the parrot had known exactly what he was saying to his arch-enemy.

'Come on through to the drawing room in twenty minutes,' Donato continued as Lorenzo walked across to Benito and gently stroked the bird's shining plumage, his face tragic. 'We are going to have drinks before dinner and I presume you do not wish to join us?'

Lorenzo's head lifted and he cast Bianca one heartfelt glance of dislike before muttering, 'No, I wish to stay here.'

'Twenty minutes, then.' Donato nodded at Grace, his dark eyes hooded. 'If you are ready. . .?'

She wasn't; she wasn't at all ready to join the others in the beautiful drawing room for social chit-chat. She would much rather stay here with Lorenzo and Benito, but she couldn't very well say so, she thought rebelliously as she followed Bianca out of the room. As usual Donato's word was law and everyone jumped to obey.

Dinner was the nightmare she had expected it to be although Cecilia's culinary skills were, as ever, first-class. The main course, *carpaccio*—a dish of paper-thin slices of fillet steak garnished with fresh egg mayonnaise and finely slivered parmesan—had been Grace's favourite when she had lived in Italy before, and she suspected *Cecilia* had made the meal with her specially in mind.

Because of that, and Bianca's piercing, eagle-eyed stare that was just waiting for any sign of weakness, she forced herself to eat everything on her plate although the delicious food tasted like sawdust in her mouth, as had the soup beforehand.

'So, it is good that you have an interesting job,' Bianca said sweetly as Grace finished the last mouthful of food, continuing the conversation that she had begun earlier when she had enquired, with almost indecent interest, about Grace's life in England. 'That you are fulfilled, happy, *si*?'

She didn't remember saying anything about being happy or fulfilled, Grace thought silently as she glanced across at the other woman without answering, her whole being tuned in to the big, dark figure to her right. Donato had said little during the meal but she had been vitally conscious of every tiny movement he had made, of his large, capable hands as he had eaten or lifted the crystal wineglass to his lips, of his cool, sardonic face and narrowed eyes.

He was fascinating, powerfully enigmatic, and it was taking all of her will-power to sustain the calm façade she was hiding behind. She had forgotten just how hypnotic his presence was, how he could reduce her to a trembling wreck with just a lift of those satanic black eyebrows, but she was remembering now all right, she thought grimly.

'And you are returning. . .when?' Bianca paused, her face innocent and her voice gentle, as though the enquiry were one of politeness, nothing more. But both women knew it was not.

'I'm not sure yet,' Grace said shortly, her voice curt.

'Grace is home for the moment,' Donato said smoothly, 'and has no immediate plans to return to England. Now, if we have all finished I suspect Anna is hovering with the dessert.'

It was a clear warning to Bianca that further questions would not be well received and his deliberate use of the word 'home' was for her benefit too, Grace thought, struggling to let nothing of what she was thinking show on her face. Well, he could insinuate all he wanted but she would not be intimidated by hints or even downright orders; she was her own mistress now and in charge of her comings and goings. And her days of trying to placate Bianca were over too!

Bianca was silent throughout the rest of the meal— something for which Grace was inordinately grateful, although the once or twice she met the Italian woman's glance across the table her flesh crept at the chilling coldness in the beautiful almond eyes even as the thin, finely modelled mouth smiled at her.

Lorenzo had eaten little and said less, his huge dark eyes fixed mostly on his plate and his thin body perfectly still, so when Gina brought the grappa—a spirit distilled from grapeskins alleged to help digestion at the end of a meal—Grace rose from the table, gesturing to the small boy as she did so.

'Lorenzo and I are both tired,' she said quietly, noting Donato's glance of surprise at her boldness with a dart of satisfaction, 'so I hope you will excuse us.' Lorenzo moved quickly to her side as she spoke and she put her arm round the narrow shoulders, hugging him against her for a brief moment. He was her main concern now, not Donato, not Bianca, not even her own fragile equilibrium.

'Of course.' Ever the gentleman, Donato rose immediately, pulling her chair back with one hand as he ruffled his brother's curls with the other, but she noticed his eyes were flint-hard as they ran over her face and surmised that he hadn't liked her decisiveness. It was a side to her he had seen only rarely in the past.

Tough, she thought tightly. There's a lot more where that came from. She wasn't the dewy-eyed, besotted little teenager he had married or the stricken, broken woman who had left this house twelve months ago. As he had so rightly intimated, she had changed. She had mourned the passing of the old Grace at the time, not at all certain if she liked the new person who had taken her place, but now, for the first time, she realised she had grown in strength and wisdom, that something positive had been formed from all the devastation. She couldn't spend all her life trying to please everyone.

'Grace?' Lorenzo plucked at her arm as they climbed the stairs to his room. 'It was not Benito's fault—the words he said to Bianca. He is only a bird; he was just repeating what the gardener had taught him,' he said defensively.

'Was it very bad?' she asked quietly, trying to keep her face straight. She had picked up a smattering of Italian during her time in Italy, although most of the Vittoria family had only spoken English in her presence—Bianca being the exception—but she had never heard the words the parrot had spoken.

Lorenzo gave her a sidelong glance which spoke volumes as his conscience wrestled with his loyalty to Benito. 'Quite bad,' he admitted after a few seconds, and then, as he gave a little sob as they reached the top of the stairs, Grace knelt down to him, taking the stiff little body into her arms.

'Hey, what's this?' It was a moment or two before he relaxed against her and then his arms snaked round her neck in a stranglehold. 'You aren't upset about Benito, are you?' she asked softly as he buried his face in her neck. 'You know he didn't mean it.'

'Bianca said he should go,' Lorenzo whispered between gulping sobs. 'She said that, did she not? And she said Madre would have wanted it. Do you think that, Grace? That Madre wants him to go?'

'You know that's rubbish, Lorenzo.' Grace stroked his hair gently. 'Your mother loved Benito; she bought him for you, didn't she? He used to make her laugh when he was naughty—'

'But Bianca *said*,' he interrupted desperately.

'I don't care what your sister said,' Grace said firmly. 'She is quite, quite wrong. Your mother loved Benito as much as you do, if not more. You know she loved him in your heart of hearts.'

'She could not love him more than me.' Lorenzo moved his head to look at her now, his deep brown eyes sparkling with tears and his mouth quivering. 'He is my best friend. If he was sent away—'

'He won't be.' The small boy continued to look at her unblinkingly and she said again, 'He won't be, Lorenzo, I promise you. *I promise you.* All right?'

'But Bianca does not like me to care so much for Benito and Benito knows; that is why he is so rude to her. What if she asks Donato to send him away?' he asked earnestly. 'I know she hates him.'

'Donato wouldn't.' And as she said it she knew he wouldn't, without a shadow of a doubt, and the knowledge bothered her. 'He loves you much too much to do that; if you don't believe me ask him,' she finished lightly. 'Now, come along to your room and pop into bed; you're very tired and no one can think straight when they're tired. Benito will never be sent away; Donato wouldn't do that.'

Once the small boy had emerged from his bathroom, washed and clad in striped blue pyjamas, Grace patted his bed on which she was sitting. 'Now come and snuggle down and I'll tell you a story if you like,' she offered with a warm smile. 'If you promise to shut your eyes and try to go to sleep.'

Making up stories for Lorenzo had become something of a bedtime ritual almost from the first evening she had lived in the house; even when Paolo had been born she had brought him along to Lorenzo's bedroom where he had lain next to his young uncle gurgling and kicking and apparently enjoying the stories too.

The image of how it had been was suddenly too painful and she forced the memories back under lock and key as she began to speak, hoping that the ruse for taking Lorenzo's mind off the forthcoming day would work and that the small boy would be able to relax into sleep.

It was ten minutes later when Donato walked into the room, and as Lorenzo sat up in bed his first words indicated that the incident before dinner was still very much on his mind. 'Grace says you would not send Benito away.' The young voice was attempting to sound confident but the thread of anxiety was unmistakable, and Donato's eyes flashed to Grace's calm face before resting on that of his young brother with tender understanding.

'And Grace is right.' He smiled a slow smile of reassurance. 'Would I send you away? Can you imagine such an idea? It is just as ridiculous to think of Benito leaving our family; he is part of it. A mischievous, troublesome part, to be sure—' the dark eyes flashed their amusement and Lorenzo's face relaxed '—but family nevertheless. Benito could not do anything that would make me send him away, Lorenzo. Trust me.'

'I do trust you, Donato.' There was a wealth of conviction in Lorenzo's voice and Grace bit her lip hard. Once she would have said the same, but not any more. 'Grace is telling me a story about a boy who has his own magic racing car.' Lorenzo was passionate about cars of all shapes and sizes. 'Do you want to listen too?' he offered magnanimously.

'This is acceptable?' Donato looked straight at her and Grace nodded shakily, summoning a cool smile from somewhere beyond herself. This was too poignant, too much like days gone by.

'Of course.' She held the glittering gaze for one moment before her eyes dropped to Lorenzo, who had curled back down under the light covers. 'Do you want to say your prayers now, before I begin again? Then if you fall asleep it won't matter,' she suggested carefully. 'You're very tired.'

'All right.' The black head nodded and as Donato seated himself in a chair facing the bed, one long leg crossed across his knee and his eyes tight on Grace's face, Lorenzo began the Lord's Prayer, finishing with, 'And please, God, look after Madre now she is with you and tell her I miss her.' There was a moment of deep silence and then he continued in a thick voice, 'But I am glad Paolo is not alone any more. He used to like to be cuddled and now Madre can cuddle him all the time.'

He said more, going on to list some of the needs in his young life in the simple, innocent way children had, but Grace's attention was focused on Donato, who had risen abruptly at his brother's words, walking to stand with his back to the room as he stared out of the window into the garden below, his big body stiff and taut and his hands thrust into the pockets of his trousers.

He continued to stand there, silent and unmoving, whilst she told Lorenzo his story, and when the child's steady, rhythmic breathing confirmed he was asleep she spoke Donato's name quietly, inclining her head towards the bedroom door when he turned to face her.

Once on the shadowed landing outside the room she

felt suddenly shy and vulnerable, a world removed from the determined woman who had led Lorenzo out of the dining room, and the feeling of susceptibility made her voice brittle as she said, 'Thank you for reassuring him about Benito; he needed to hear it from your mouth, I think. The parrot is more than a parrot as far as he is concerned.'

'The parrot is more than a parrot as far as anyone is concerned,' Donato said drily, his voice dark and sardonic.

'You can't blame Benito for sticking up for himself,' Grace began hotly, only to stop abruptly as she realised how ridiculous she sounded.

'You see?' Donato leant against the far wall as he surveyed her with narrowed eyes, his big, lean body relaxed and his arms crossed over his broad chest. 'You are doing it yourself, are you not—attributing human qualities to the bird? You know as well as I do that Benito was quite aware of the meaning of the words he aimed at Bianca. That parrot is a match for any of us.'

'Even if that's so—and I'm not saying I think it is,' she added hastily, 'Bianca deserved it.'

'Hmm.' Donato levered himself upright, his voice dark with concealed amusement. 'Well, leaving aside the physical impossibility of what Benito suggested, his language was not at all what I would wish for a young child's ears. However—' he stopped the protest she was about to make with an upraised hand '—I do concede that the parrot is more sinned against than sinful. In this instance.'

'Exactly.' She was more than thankful he was taking such a reasonable line and it showed in her voice, causing the coal-black eyes to fasten more intently on her face.

'You did not think I would see things this way?' Donato asked softly. 'You thought Benito's future was precarious?'

'On the contrary, I knew you would do nothing to upset Lorenzo,' she protested quickly. 'I never thought for a minute you would consider sending the parrot away;

you understand Lorenzo too well. . .' Her voice trailed away as he moved closer to stand just in front of her, his tanned face still and expressionless and the intensity in the heavily lashed eyes unnerving.

'But you—you I do not understand at all,' he said quietly. 'I could accept the need to get away for a time, from the memories that were ever present in this house, from the heartache, the pain, from. . .me. But now—now it would seem this time has not healed anything. This is true, is it not?'

'And you really thought it would?' she said with a bitterness she was powerless to hide. 'That I could just forget the past?'

'You cannot live in the past for ever, Grace,' he said softly. 'Neither can you exist indefinitely in the glass bubble you have made for yourself; I will not let you for one thing.'

'Donato—'

'We need to talk about what has happened. Painful though it will be, the wound needs to be cauterised—'

'No!' He expected her to sit down with him and actually *discuss* his affair with Maria? she asked herself incredulously. After all this time, all the months of aching loneliness and desperate learning to do without him, he thought that just because she happened to be back in his environment again, within his reach, he could click his fingers and explain away his betrayal with a few well-chosen words so she would share his bed? Because that was what all this boiled down to in the cold light of day. The male sex drive.

'I have nothing to say to you, Donato,' she stated slowly, a painful finality in every syllable. 'It is too late.'

'This is not true and it is unacceptable.' The softness had gone from his voice, replaced by a hard, cold determination that was all Vittoria. '"Too late" does not feature in my vocabulary.'

'I don't—'

'You have known me for five years and lived with me for a good proportion of that time,' he continued ruthlessly, ignoring her weak protest as though she had not spoken. 'You know I always get what I want in the end, Grace, and I have wanted you from the first moment I laid eyes on you. I have no intention of relinquishing my rights and this you must understand.'

'You have no rights,' she objected hotly. 'You waved them all aside and you know it, and no court in the land would say differently. How can you—?'

'Donato?' Bianca's voice was loud and penetrating, slicing through the heated exchange like cold steel and bringing both their heads swinging to the staircase at the end of the landing. 'Donato? Is anything wrong? Is Lorenzo all right?'

'*Damn it!*' The words were savage and his eyes didn't leave her flushed face even when the sound of Bianca's footsteps could be heard up the stairs. As the Italian woman came into view it was Grace who broke the contact, by taking a step backwards and turning away, praying the trembling deep in the pit of her stomach had not revealed itself to those piercingly intuitive eyes. He saw too much, he always had, but whereas once his discernment where she was concerned had been welcome, reassuring even, now it was a danger she had to guard against every moment.

Grace called on all the will-power she possessed as she walked towards Bianca, who had paused at the sight of them, her slanted gaze sharp and speculative before she schooled her features into the sweet, innocent mask she normally adopted in the presence of her brother.

'We were worried.' One slim, beautifully manicured hand fluttered gracefully as she indicated the floor below where Romano was waiting. 'Lorenzo ate so little, we thought maybe he had a bad stomach. *Si?* Poor little boy.'

'No, he does not have stomach ache.' Donato's voice just behind Grace was harsh and cold. 'He was concerned about Benito, that is all, and I will have no further suggestions of the kind you made before dinner, Bianca. Is that clear? The parrot is here to stay, for better or worse, and that is final.'

'Of course.' Bianca's eyes opened wide with simulated surprise and her voice was apologetic and soft. 'I did not seriously mean what I said, Donato; you surely know this? I do not care for the creature myself but Lorenzo is inordinately attached to it. I was concerned for Lorenzo's health, that is all, and perhaps his moral standards. It is not good for him to hear such obscenities and this needs to be impressed upon Lorenzo as well as the bird, *si*?' She smiled understandingly, her eyes wide and innocent.

'I think Lorenzo will hear a lot worse in the course of his life,' Donato said drily, 'but I take your point. However, one can hardly take a parrot to task for merely repeating what he has been taught. Steps were taken with the perpetrator—' a thread of steel had briefly entered his voice and Grace felt a dart of sympathy for the unfortunate gardener '—and that is the end of the matter.'

The last words were a direct warning, and in spite of her pretence at concern and consideration for her young brother Bianca's wrath at being reprimanded in front of Grace showed through for an instant in the darkness of her face before she recovered herself and took Donato's arm with a trembling smile.

'Oh, dear, the storm—how do you say it—in the teacup?' she murmured gently, her face managing to portray sadness and brave wistfulness in the same instant. 'I am so concerned that Lorenzo remembers the values Madre taught him, that he grows strong and true in the traditions of the Vittorias. Madre loved him so much. I feel... responsible to see this is so.'

Clever, very clever, Grace thought silently as she followed the other two downstairs, Bianca managing to hold onto Donato's arm in such a way that it would have been discourteous for him to attempt to extricate himself from his sister's grasp.

She didn't believe for a moment that Bianca had been considering Lorenzo or anyone else in her attack on the bane of her life; she thoroughly disliked the parrot and had seized an opportunity to plant the seeds for his dismissal in Donato's mind. The blame for the fact that it had all misfired would no doubt be laid at her door in the other woman's mind, but she didn't care; Lorenzo was the only one who mattered in all this. She was done with trying to pacify and befriend Bianca; that had all finished one day twelve months ago when she had seen the pleasure in the other woman's face as she had spat her venom with deadly accuracy.

Once in the hall Donato paused, turning to face her as she joined them, Bianca still hanging onto his arm like a limpet. 'You will join us for coffee?' he asked flatly, his expression unchanging as she shook her head quickly.

'No, I don't think so. If you'll excuse me I really am very tired,' she said politely, but with a firmness that was unmistakable.

'Of course.' He bowed slightly as he spoke, his face remote and cold, and just for a moment incredulity that they had come to such a pass swept over her again, turning her eyes dark and cloudy. 'Goodnight, Grace.'

'Goodnight.' He had already turned away before she answered but as the word left her lips Bianca turned, her voice light and charming as she said her own goodnight, the tone at strict variance with the look in her slanted eyes, which was savage and black and as satanic as hell itself.

CHAPTER FIVE

'Two weeks...' Grace murmured sleepily as she lay watching a sunbeam dancing through the drifting lace curtains, the vastness of the bed Donato had insisted on buying for their marital bedroom dwarfing her small shape. She had been in Italy two weeks now and the days had been bitter-sweet, a mixture of pain and pleasure she couldn't have explained to anyone. The funeral had been traumatic but Lorenzo had surprised her with his maturity, his tight control and dignified grief proving Donato right again in his belief that his young brother should be allowed to attend.

Donato ... She rolled over on to her stomach but the trembling excitement and apprehension that the thought of him produced banished the last remnants of drowsiness in spite of the early hour, and after a few minutes of tossing and turning she sat up abruptly, her brow wrinkling in a frown as she rolled irritably out of bed.

She ought to be pleased he had shown nothing but cool restraint since that first night back under Casa Pontina's roof, and she was, *she was*, she told herself firmly, letting the soft, silky shower water flow over her smooth skin, which was already turning a glowing honey-gold. It was just that...

Oh, she didn't know what it was, she admitted testily, reaching for the shampoo and massaging her scalp with far more force than was necessary. What was the title of that old song? Something about washing a man right out of her hair? If only it were that simple!

She was ready long before breakfast, sitting in the warm May sunlight on the balcony and idly sipping a cold glass of sparkling mineral water from the small fridge in her bedroom as she contemplated the forthcoming day. Donato had suggested the evening before, his voice remote and his manner distant, that she and Lorenzo might enjoy a drive down the coast to Amalfi, where some friends of his lived whose eldest son was the same age as Lorenzo. Lorenzo had been so pleased at the thought of visiting Giuseppe that she hadn't had the heart to refuse, although the thought of a day spent in close proximity to Donato had made her feel. . .odd.

But that was natural, perfectly natural in the circumstances, she told herself reassuringly, her gaze wandering over the beautifully tended grounds beneath a sky of shimmering azure-blue. She had been married to the man, for goodness' sake; well. . .she still was. She forbade her mind to continue down that path and conjure up the intimate details that haunted her dreams and plagued her days, but it was difficult, and becoming more so.

Why did he have to be so attractive? she asked herself desperately, standing up and smoothing her white denim jeans over her hips before tucking her white sleeveless top more securely in the waistband. But that was all it was—attractiveness. Physical appeal. Sexual magnetism. Lust. Call it what you will, it didn't mean anything, not really.

That comforting argument was put severely to the test when she entered the breakfast room some minutes later to find Donato already in occupancy. The tall, broad-shouldered body was clothed casually in black denim jeans and shirt which accentuated his dark good looks even more, underlining the hard male strength and power in a frame that was unequivocally masculine.

She felt her senses leap as the jet-black eyes narrowed on her face and there was something burning in their depths that brought a flush to her face as she forced a polite greeting. 'Good morning.' She hoped her voice betrayed none of the nervousness that had plagued her since waking.

'Innocent and untouched.'

'What?' She paused in the act of lifting the lid of one of the covered dishes on the massive sideboard that stretched down one side of the room, and glanced across at him, thinking she must have misheard the deep, lazy murmur.

'Innocent and untouched—the way you look this morning,' he drawled slowly, putting the paper he had been reading to one side and leaning back in his chair to survey her better. 'Especially clad in virginal white.'

There was deep sexual knowledge smouldering in the dark eyes, a hunger and desire that told her he was remembering only too well the blazing passion that used to consume them both with their first touch of each other, and as she felt her body stir shamefully, her breasts tightening and hardening in response to her thoughts, she forced her panicky heartbeat to slow and took a long, deep, hidden breath.

'Looks are deceptive, as we both know,' she said with brittle brightness. 'I'm neither innocent nor untouched and. . .and having had a baby certainly not virginal by any stretch of the imagination.'

She had had to force herself to go on, to speak of Paolo's birth with some degree of naturalness, but having done so she felt an overwhelming sense of relief that at last it was becoming easier.

He said nothing as he continued to sit there but the dark gaze had turned heart-wrenchingly tender, which told her he understood, and it made her want to cry. And cry. And cry. And to combat the weakness, the terribly seductive weakness that had her wanting to throw herself into his arms and take anything he wanted to give, on any terms, she continued, 'Neither am I, as you so rightly pointed out when I arrived, anything like the girl you once knew. We've both changed, Donato, irrevocably.' She raised her chin as she spoke, her eyes daring him to disagree.

'That is a harsh word and I never thought of you as harsh,' he said quietly, but the tenderness had died and although she felt a moment's pain she was glad. She could cope with Donato Vittoria as hard, arrogant monarch, lord of his own little kingdom where his word was law and he imposed it ruthlessly; she could handle that, albeit with difficulty now and then. And any time she felt herself begin to slide down the slippery slope of regrets and memories she only had to think about a certain female form, with long black hair and golden-brown eyes, for the ground to be firm under her feet once more.

'Like I said, I've changed,' she said firmly. 'I had to start again when I got back to England, and I know what I want from life now, who I am and where I'm going.' She expected him to challenge such a statement but the hard mask he normally showed the world was in place now and he merely smiled, a cold; slightly cruel smile that sent a shiver down her spine.

'A woman who knows exactly what she wants,' he drawled silkily. 'Certainly formidable to the average male, but then, I am not the average male, *mia piccola*, or had you forgotten? Perhaps I prefer the full-grown cat with claws to the playful little kitten?' he finished with smooth insolence.

'I don't care what you prefer,' she snapped quickly, stung by his cool equanimity as much as by the barbed smile.

'No?' The chilling smile deepened. 'But that makes it even more stimulating, would you not agree? We must pursue this conversation further, but as I hear Lorenzo approaching now is not the time.'

'Never will be the time,' she flashed back, her cheeks burning and her eyes blazing, only for him to raise his eyebrows in dark mockery of her outrage before turning his head to smile at Lorenzo as he appeared in the open doorway.

'Looking forward to seeing Giuseppe?' Donato asked his small brother, with a warm smile that was in direct contrast to the one he had given Grace a few moments before. 'You look as though you are going for a week instead of a day,' he added drily, indicating the large, bulging travel bag Lorenzo was holding with both hands, its weight making the thin frame bend right over.

'I am taking some of my computer games and my joy-stick,' Lorenzo said earnestly, 'so we can play on

Giuseppe's game console, and my new car books, and my army figures— Oh, good morning, Grace,' he said quickly as he caught sight of her for the first time. 'You look nice,' he added with a wide smile.

'That is just what I said.' Donato's voice was perfectly bland and she could have hit him, but he gave her no chance to make any comment as he continued, 'I trust you have your bathing clothes in the bag so you can play in Giuseppe's pool? Grace and I will not be around for part of the day as we are visiting Salerno. It is something we always planned to do in the past but never accomplished, and as the town is of great historical interest with its medieval centre it would be good for Grace to see, do you not agree?'

Lorenzo was obviously gratified at his opinion being sought and nodded enthusiastically, leaving Grace in the difficult position of either objecting, and so revealing to Lorenzo that relations between her and Donato were not as harmonious as the small boy thought, or allowing Donato to manipulate both her and the day to his own advantage. She decided the latter was the lesser of two evils and contented herself with one acid glance at Donato when Lorenzo was busy helping himself to scrambled eggs, to which he responded with lifted brows, wide, innocent eyes and an irritatingly satisfied smile.

The man was a monster, she thought balefully as she forced down a bowl of freshly sliced grapefruit and two slices of toast, ever conscious of the dark, solid presence opposite. Arrogant, high-handed, overbearing... He made her so *mad*; how could she ever have imagined herself in love with him?

She raised her eyes for an instant and met the wry, crooked smile across the table that told her he was quite aware of her vitriolic thoughts, and also reminded her exactly why she had loved him so much. She bit down hard on her full lower lip, applied herself steadfastly to the toast and didn't raise her eyes from her plate again.

At least he was dressed this morning, she thought thankfully as she finished the last bite of toast and reached for her coffee-cup. She had forgotten Donato's preference for dressing after breakfast and the first morning after the funeral, when she had come through to the main house and walked blithely into the breakfast room, she had suffered a terrific jolt to the system. He had been sitting at the table, totally relaxed, the big male body naked except for a short grey silk robe that had been knotted with careless—frighteningly careless—unconcern.

She had caught a glimpse of thick black curls on the broad, muscled chest, forced her gaze upwards to where his cool, dark eyes had been watching her obvious confusion with satisfied amusement, and called on all the resources she possessed to force her trembling legs to walk across the room. Dressed, his virile masculinity was intimidating; almost naked, it was overwhelmingly powerful, and breakfast-time had become a subtle torture that she just couldn't seem to take in her stride no matter how she primed herself beforehand.

But it had been better this morning—fractionally— although it seemed her body was destined to respond to his in a way she could well have done without.

'I thought we would leave about nine, if that is convenient?' He spoke with formal politeness, in the same way he had conducted all their conversations over the last two weeks, but as she inclined her head and met the narrowed gaze head-on she saw that the fire that had blazed into life that morning was still there in the dark eyes, merely banked down a little at the moment.

And yet he had been so distant since the confrontation on the night of her arrival. Had it all been an act? And, if so, why? Or was he merely toying with her, playing hot and cold for some obscure reason of his own? She didn't know; she didn't understand him and she didn't want to. End of story.

The words mocked her as she walked out of the front door just after nine and saw him leaning nonchalantly against the side of the white BMW he used when he wanted to drive himself; Lorenzo was already perched on the back seat, the big bag by his side.

The brilliant sunshine suddenly put the white car and dark-haired figure all clothed in black into stark monochrome, causing her to blink uncertainly as the image became all-consuming, threatening, causing her hand to flutter to her throat in protest.

'Grace?' Something of what she was feeling must have shown in her face because in two bounds he was beside her, taking her arm as he turned her slightly to face him. 'What is it? You look as though you have seen a ghost.' His hand was warm and solid on her flesh, the enticing scent of his aftershave reassuringly familiar, and it brought her back from the edge of panic although the underlying feeling that had caused her alarm remained. She had felt, just for a second, the same way a little animal must feel in the horrifying moment after it has walked into a trap set by a vastly superior predator from which there is no escape. But there *was* an escape for her, she told herself shakily, in fact she had already made it.

'I just felt faint for a moment.' She forced the words through lips that tried to smile but couldn't. 'It must be the heat. I'm still not used to it after the drizzle and rain in England.'

'You would prefer to stay at home?' Yes, she would, she most certainly would. But Lorenzo's little face peering anxiously out of the window settled the matter. He came first, her feelings came second.

'No, I'm fine now.' This time the smile came and held. 'Lorenzo would be disappointed and he is doing so well. He's so much better, don't you think? Children adapt so quickly.'

Donato stared at her for a full thirty seconds without speaking, his hard, handsome face revealing that he was quite aware of the hidden meaning behind her words, and his voice was quiet and deep, with a steel-like hardness, when he replied, 'He still needs you here, Grace.

You know it and so do I, so do not pretend differently. You are not able to run away yet.'

'Run away?' The outrage she felt scalded the last vestige of weakness out of her system. 'I don't know what you're talking about,' she said hotly. 'I came here of my own free will, if you remember, and I'm staying for Lorenzo in spite of having a job on hold in England and besides other commitments.'

'We are very grateful.' It was said with cutting sarcasm.

'And so you should be,' she flashed back bitterly. 'You don't think I enjoy being here, do you? I hate it. I hate *you*.' It was said with a desperate need to convince herself as well as him, and in the second before the angry ebony eyes iced over she thought she saw a flash of pain, but it was gone so quickly she knew she had to be mistaken. It had been a trick of the light, nothing more.

'You will be quiet,' he said in a frosty undertone that was totally devoid of any expression whatsoever. 'I will not have Lorenzo disturbed by your inability to control yourself, is that clear? What you think about me is your own concern, but you will not burden a small boy with the knowledge. I thought better of you, Grace,' he finished grimly in a tone one might have used to an errant child.

For a moment she felt three instead of twenty-three, and it didn't help that she knew Donato was right; she was behaving badly. Fortunately Donato had shielded her from Lorenzo's gaze, and the fact that the car stereo was on and had made their conversation inaudible to the small boy was more luck than judgement on her part. She bit her lip, forcing herself to calm down.

What was happening to her? she asked herself helplessly. She never behaved like this normally but the words had burst forth before she'd had time to stop them and it frightened her. 'I'm sorry.' She suddenly wanted to cry but she would rather have died than let him know. 'I shouldn't have said all that.'

She had no idea how delicate and ethereal she appeared

to the big, dark man looking down at her, or that her
mouth was faintly tremulous and her eyes dark with confusion. So it came as a complete surprise when in the
next instant he drew her against the hard wall of his chest
for a few heart-stopping moments, his voice deep and
soft as he said, 'You are tearing yourself apart, *mia piccola*, and all to no avail.'

She had no time to react before he had put her from
him and was leading her down the steps, his face set in
the dark, autocratic mask she knew so well, but once in
the car she found she was shaking—and not just due
to the angry exchange of words.

She wanted him. Physically she wanted him very
much, and each day spent at Casa Pontina was making
it worse. When he had held her close for those few
seconds the intensity of her searing response to the feel
and touch and smell of him had shocked her more than
she could believe.

She wanted to feel his hands and mouth on every part
of her body again, stroking her, caressing her, exciting
her to vibrant life until she was moist and quivering
beneath him, ready for the final act of possession, and it
was that secret realisation, which she had been fighting
every second of every day and night—oh, especially the
nights—since she had been back, that was sending her
half-mad.

Because, along with the memory of how it had been,
another one was seared on the screen of her mind—that
of Donato and Maria together, their bodies entwined and
joined and burning with the heat of shared passion. Had
he told her he loved her? The thought wasn't new to
Grace but still had the power to turn her insides to melted
jelly. Probably, very probably, she thought wretchedly.
They had had it all and now they had nothing.

Grace said little on the drive to Amalfi, but her quiet-
ness wasn't obvious as Donato kept up a lively
conversation with Lorenzo. She felt Donato's keen
glance sweep across her face more than once but kept

her eyes on the changing view outside the car window as she battled with her emotions.

He could laugh and joke with Lorenzo as though he hadn't a care in the world, and he probably hadn't, she thought bitterly, whereas her nerves were stretched as tight as piano wire. *He* had betrayed *her* and she was the one still suffering for it. It wasn't fair. Life just wasn't fair. And she might be indulging in morbid self-pity, she thought militantly, but for once she didn't care.

When they arrived at Donato's friend's home, a charming villa perfectly suited to the enchanting and truly Italian town of Amalfi, Grace found another shock in store. She had met Alessandro and Anna a couple of times before and had liked both them and Giuseppe, a serious little boy with deep brown hair and liquid brown eyes, but, on walking into a shady courtyard, protected from the fierce Italian sun by a canopy of luxuriant foliage and bordered by old magnolia trees and a semi-circle of flowering oleanders, she found someone else in residence.

'This is Emanuele.' Donato whisked the six-month-old baby boy out of Anna's arms as he spoke once the initial greetings were over. 'Manuele for short.' Although he was holding the baby his eyes were fixed tight on Grace's white face, and she knew he had registered the bolt of panic and shock that had run her through on their arrival. 'Here.'

He'd done this on purpose. The thought was paramount even as her arms opened instinctively to receive the child Donato placed quickly in her arms without giving her any chance to object. After Paolo's death she had found it too painful to come into contact with babies—any babies—and she hadn't held one since the last time she had cradled Paolo, tears streaming down her face, just before they had come to take him away.

She was vaguely aware of Anna hustling the two boys into the villa, leaving her and Donato alone in the sweetly scented silence, and of Donato gently seating her in a big cushioned cane chair, but her whole being was taken up with the sleeping child nestled in her lap, who hadn't stirred despite his rapid delivery from one pair of arms to another.

He was beautiful. She gazed at the thick eyelashes curling on plump, soft baby cheeks and at the small hand on which a dimpled chin was resting, minute fingernails transparently delicate. So beautiful. Paolo, oh, Paolo. . .

'We shall see him again.' Donato's voice was thick and husky, and as she raised her head she saw his face, too, was wet.

'Do you believe that?' she whispered brokenly. 'Really believe it?'

'With all my heart.' His hand reached out and stroked a black curl off the baby's forehead. 'One day we shall be reunited and this life will seem but the blink of an eye, a moment of time, but in the meantime it is here to be lived.'

'And you think I'm not—living, that is?' she asked slowly. 'Is that why you planned this?'

'Partly.' He didn't try to pretend he didn't know what she meant, or excuse himself in any way, although his legs were weak with relief that she had taken it so well. It had been a gamble, but then, what wasn't?

She stared at him for a moment, her mind racing, before she lowered her gaze to the baby who was beginning to stir. You had to be cruel to be kind. The old adage was truer than most and, knowing Donato as she did, she knew he would never flinch from what he thought was right, ruthless though it might be. She sat quite still, her mind and senses adjusting to the baby smell and feel of the child, and he was wise enough to say and do no more until Anna came out with a tray of coffee and normal social intercourse was resumed.

'Are you sure you won't stay for lunch?' Anna pressed as Donato rose after a few minutes, drawing Grace up with him.

'Not this time.' Donato smiled the rare but fascinating smile that lit his dark face like a ray of sunshine and never failed to mesmerise those fortunate enough to witness the metamorphosis. 'We will be back in time for dinner and I look forward to seeing Alessandro then. Is he still working too hard?'

'Always.' Anna rolled her eyes heavenwards as she moved her hands in a Latin gesture of despair, following them out to the car with Emanuele now securely tucked in her arms with his nappy-clad bottom resting on one hip in a way mothers have carried their children from the beginning of time.

It hurt to see the bright-eyed, black-haired little boy who was so like Paolo, but the pain was more poignant than agonising, unlike the searing white-hot torment that had sent her half-mad in the early days. Nevertheless Grace was glad when they turned the corner and the villa was lost from sight, and as a sudden thought occurred to her she turned to Donato, touching his arm tentatively for a moment. 'Is Manuele the reason you didn't want to stay at the villa with Lorenzo all day?' she asked softly. 'You thought it would be too much for me?'

He glanced at her swiftly before concentrating on the road again. 'Partly.' His voice was cool, careful.

'But why? Why suggest we go there in the first place, then?' she asked, bewildered. 'We didn't have to go.'

'Lorenzo needed the company of another child for a few hours,' Donato said expressionlessly. 'And it was also time.'

'Time?' She stared at the hard, handsome profile uncertainly.

'Time to face Manuele and all the other Manueles,' he said quietly. 'Besides which, as I said, Manuele was only partly the reason I did not wish to spend the day with Anna and the boys.' He glanced at her again, his eyes dark and burning hot as they washed over her pale fragility. 'Can you not think of another reason, *mia piccola*? Why I might want to be alone with my wife for a few hours? Surely that is natural in a husband?'

'Don't.' The tumult of feeling that had coursed through her at the husky note in his voice terrified her. 'Don't say that.'

'But it is true.' He smiled mirthlessly. 'Odious though the thought is to you, the fact remains that you are my wife, Grace, and we have been apart for twelve months.'

'And whose fault is that?' she returned bitterly. 'You—'

'No more—say no more.' His voice was hard now, sharp, and the tone cut off her protest in mid-flow. 'I do not intend to have a day that is spent quarrelling with you,' he said tightly, 'this is not good for either of us. For the sake of what once was, this day will be a—how you say?—truce? Is that the right word?'

'Yes.' She sat quite still, her hands clasped in her lap now and her body stiff, her heart thudding against her ribs so hard she felt her chest would explode. She didn't want to spend a day with him under a flag of armistice, she acknowledged silently. She was too frightened. Not of him—no, it was more than that. She was distrustful of herself, scared of how she would be if she let her guard down for one moment.

Oh. . . She shut her eyes for a split second as self-contempt burnt hotly through her limbs. What was she? Woman or mouse? Where was her backbone, her belief in her own character? By his own words he had informed her that he knew exactly how she viewed him, and there was no question that he didn't understand she considered their relationship over. And surely for the sake of Paolo, for the life they had created, she could endure one day of tentative cease-fire in their warring relationship.

'All right.' She didn't see the hard-muscled body sag for just an infinitesimal moment before straightening immediately when she spoke. 'A truce, just for today. Friends.'

'Friends?' His voice was deep, husky, and she shivered at its seductive power even as she kept herself quiet and still. 'Ah, now that is something else again, *mia piccola*.' She saw the hard profile twist in a smile before he continued, 'But enough talking. We will eat and then I will show you Salerno, *sì*? And later we will drive to a little cove I know and bathe in that blue sea you look at so longingly.'

It was true, she had been looking at the deep sapphire water and wishing she could let it cool her overheated body, but not right now, in the company of Donato, and certainly not at this 'little cove' he mentioned. She remembered the knack he had had in the past of finding deserted little bays where it had seemed as if they were the only two people alive in all the world, and she also remembered what had invariably followed once they had left the water to lie on the warm powdery sand, with the blue sky above and the turquoise sea lapping gently in the background.

The memory prompted her to say, with more urgency than tact, 'Oh, no——no. We can't swim. I haven't brought my costume or towels, for one thing, and we'll have to get back for dinner. It wouldn't be fair to keep Anna waiting,' she added breathlessly.

'Indeed not,' he agreed smoothly, the silky note in his voice telling her he was quite aware of her unease and the reason for it. 'But I had the foresight to pack the necessary bathing kit this morning, and there will be plenty of time before we are due back. Now, lunch and then the cathedral first, I think. The early thirteenth-century Romanesque bell tower you will particularly enjoy, and some of the works of art in the church are quite breathtaking,' he continued coolly, as though he wasn't aware he was riding rough-shod over her objections.

But he was. She sneaked a glance at the autocratic face from under her eyelashes. Oh, yes, he knew all right, and she had the distinct feeling he was less interested in showing her the medieval centre of Salerno than in the proposed swim afterwards.

Nevertheless, after lunch in one of the tiny cafés dotted about the ancient narrow alleyways and side-streets of the city, she found she was enjoying the time to wander and explore. Perhaps a little too much? she asked herself wryly, well aware that Donato had set out to present himself as charming companion and guide. A truce. She considered the word as they passed through the main entrance to the large atrium, flanked by two imposing lions. Well, yes, possibly. But a truce only went so far, at least as far as she was concerned.

They returned to the car in the heat of the afternoon and by that time any thought of objecting to a swim in the crystalline waters she had glimpsed on her way to Salerno had long since evaporated—along with most of her body fluid, Grace reflected weakly. The sun was fiercely hot in a sky of vivid blue, and the heat shimmered off buildings and roads alike, in spite of the fact it was only early May. An unusual heatwave over the last few days had taken the temperatures soaring to those normally expected in July and August, and in the narrow streets the heat was stifling.

Donato seemed quite unaffected by the weather, however, his dark good looks as cool and tranquil as always, his manner unruffled and controlled. Grace glanced at him as she collapsed feebly in her seat in the sauna that was the car, more irritated than she could express at his refusal to be dominated by the extreme conditions.

'Aren't you too hot?' she murmured exasperatedly after he had closed her door and walked round the bonnet to join her in the car. 'I mean, it's *baking*.' His effortless mastery of both himself and his environment was somehow intrinsically linked in her mind with his rejection of her.

'It is your fair English skin.' He cast her one long glance from amused eyes that acknowledged her peevishness. 'You have not had time to acclimatise yet, that is all,' he said easily.

'Acclimatise? Huh!' She desperately needed to get under his skin although she couldn't have explained why. 'Knowing my luck, I shall have just got it right when I go back,' she said irritably, watching the effect of her remark from under her eyelashes. 'And no doubt there'll be thunderstorms and rain at home.'

'Possibly,' he agreed laconically, and in a tone that

indicated he didn't care much one way or the other. 'You will be cooler once we are on the move,' he added expressionlessly, starting the engine as he spoke, his eyes veiled. 'So just be patient.'

So he had accepted her intention to return to England in the near future? she thought warily, waiting for a burst of relief that did not materialise. Instead the emotion filling her chest cavity was one of stark rejection and pain, and it horrified her.

Fool, fool, fool. She sat in dumb misery as the car gathered speed. What had she expected, for goodness' sake? Vows of undying love? Wild promises for the future? The possibility that he would abase himself, tell her he needed her, couldn't live without her? That Maria had been a mistake he was desperately sorry for?

Her hands were clenched tightly in her lap as they left Salerno and headed along the coast road, and she didn't feel the warm breeze on her face from the open window. Donato was a proud and discriminating man, possessed of both high intelligence and intimidating iron control. He also had a sexual magnetism that was undeniable and drew women like bees to a honey-pot. He didn't need to beg her to stay; he could have any woman he wanted with just a lift of his little finger. She knew that. *She knew it.*

She breathed in deeply and willed herself to relax. Even if Maria wasn't still on the scene undoubtedly another svelte young beauty had taken her place. Donato was a very physical man with a healthy sexual appetite.

'You look like one of the seven dwarfs—Grumpy, to be exact.' She was so deep in thought that the cool, lazy voice at her side almost made her jump out of her skin. 'What is it that makes you frown so fiercely, *mia piccola*?' he asked quietly. 'It is most. . .formidable.'

It was on the tip of her tongue to tell him not to use the old endearment, but she bit back the words with painful determination. She had to give the impression of being immune to that devastating Vittoria charm, difficult though that might be, and however hard it proved she was blowed if she would give that jumbo-size ego any more reason to swell. He could call her anything he liked, she told herself firmly. It was water off a duck's back.

'Well? What have I done wrong now?' he pressed softly, flashing one swift glance at her tight face from ebony-dark eyes.

'You?' She forced a light laugh that should have sounded amused and faintly patronising but merely sounded...forced. 'Whatever makes you assume I was thinking about you?' she asked stiffly. 'I could have been thinking about anything under the sun.'

'Something about the daunting set to your mouth,' he answered slowly. 'It is a shame, really, because normally it is such a nice mouth—a mouth that begs to be kissed, that promises a glimpse of heaven—'

'Don't!' Her voice was taut and sharp but he continued as though she hadn't spoken, the low husky drawl a powerfully seductive weapon in itself.

'And your skin, so rich and creamy and soft, with a scent all of its own that owes nothing to artifice. I have missed waking up in the mornings and burying myself in that enchanting perfume, Grace, caressing you awake, stroking you to life until you are moist and ripe—'

'I said stop it!' This time she jerked round in her seat to face the hard, cool profile, the creamy skin of which he had spoken searingly hot. How could he induce this tumult of feeling inside her with just a few casually spoken words when he wasn't even *touching* her?

But he was nothing if not a brilliant strategist, she told herself with painful clarity. They'd only had to touch each other in the past for a sensual voluptuousness to consume them both with such savage passion that she had sometimes thought she would die from it. And now he was painting pictures on the screen of her mind, probing those hidden desires she had fought against for twelve long months, and—Oh, God, help me, she prayed desperately—her body was there with him, every inch of the way.

'I cannot talk of these things?' he asked steadily, his

voice deep and soft. 'Why is this? Because you are frightened of what you really feel, Grace? Because you are hiding behind this oh, so high wall you have built between us?'

'There's more to a relationship than sex,' she shot back with a fierce defensiveness that caused his mouth to harden.

'A relationship?' he queried with silky control. 'You mean a marriage, surely, *mia piccola*? I am your husband.'

'No!' He glanced at her for one moment and she felt a bolt of lightning shoot through her at the black light in his glittering eyes. 'No,' she repeated weakly, 'not any more.'

'But, yes—and you want me. You want me very badly,' he stated with bald arrogance. 'And if you deny it I shall know you are lying.'

'I. . .I don't want to discuss this,' she said a trifle desperately. 'You said a truce, didn't you? A truce for today.'

'That I did.' His mouth twisted in a wry smile. 'And being the woman you are you intend to hold me to it?'

'Of course.' She didn't trust the sudden indulgence in his voice and eyed him warily from under her lashes, her violet-blue eyes guarded. 'We made a deal.'

'*Si*, I should have known.' They had been travelling down a narrow twisting lane off the main road that to Grace hadn't seemed wide enough to take the powerful BMW, but now, as Donato finished speaking, the car drew to a standstill and she saw a hidden cove in front of her: gently sloping volcanic sand leading to a bay of warm, beautifully clear blue water.

'Oh. . .' She glanced back from the scintillatingly crystal sea to Donato and found he was watching her closely, his eyes narrowed and his face expressionless. 'It's beautiful, magical.'

'And private.' His eyes mocked her, but before she could say anything he was out of the car, walking round and opening her door as he said, 'Come on, we cannot be too long indulging ourselves. Anna is cooking dinner, remember.'

He was reminding her of her earlier protestations but she chose to ignore it, her whole being taken up with the alarming fact that she was going to have to strip off in front of him to don the bikini he had so thoughtfully brought for her! He was already undoing the buttons of his denim shirt, patently unconcerned as he tugged the material out of the waistband of his jeans and pulled it off over his hairy muscled chest before his other garments followed a second later.

He was doing this on purpose! She knew he was challenging her with his brazen disregard of his nakedness, but for the life of her she couldn't look away. He was magnificent. She had forgotten just how flagrantly male he was, but now, as her eyes gazed in fascinated admiration, she felt utterly helpless and a flood of sexual excitement coursed through her veins.

'Grace?' His voice was soft and deep and sent a shiver down her spine.

'Yes?' She raised her drowning gaze to his, and to her chagrin saw dark amusement in the ebony eyes.

'You are going to change?' he asked with deceptive innocence.

'I. . .' Oh, pull yourself together—say something coherent, do something, she told her mesmerised body as she struggled to distance herself from the lithe, tanned frame in front of her. 'Yes, of course,' she said weakly. 'I. . .I'll change now.'

She climbed out of the car on trembling legs, brushing past him and reaching into the back seat for the bag holding her bikini and towels. But even with her back to him her mind was full off the broad, hard male torso and muscled limbs, the flat belly that led down to the dark circle enclosing his manhood. He wanted her. He wanted her now. His body had left her in no doubt as to his physical need, but physical desire wasn't enough, she told herself shakily. It wasn't, and she mustn't let it be.

She didn't dare turn round again, fumbling with the

bag as she pulled the brief black bikini from its depths along with two thick, fluffy beach towels. 'I can't find your trunks here,' she said jerkily, shaking the towels over the seat to see if they had got folded up inside.

'You won't.' The dark voice was unforgivably amused. 'I did not bring any.'

'Oh!' She was shocked into turning to face him again, and then wished with all her heart she hadn't. 'But. . . what if someone comes? I mean, what will you do. . .?' Her voice trailed away as he shrugged magnificent shoulders.

'No one will come, Grace.' His eyes took in her blushing confusion, relishing it. 'Did you not notice this is a private road? It belongs to the house at the top of the lane which is owned by an employee of mine—my financial director.' He smiled a predatory smile. 'And the only way one can reach the bay is by this road. So you see, you need not be fearful for my modesty.'

He had planned this. All along he had known he was going to bring her here, to this enchanting, idyllic little bay, with its powdery beach and turquoise water, she thought balefully. And why? Well, she had a pretty good idea why! But if he thought this was going to be the big seduction scene he had another think coming, she determined furiously. He might think he was irresistible to every woman from sixteen to sixty, but that giant male ego was in for a shock.

'I see.' From resources she hadn't known she possessed she forced a cool smile before turning back to the car. 'No problem, then,' she said lightly, even as her face glowed red.

'No problem,' he agreed gravely, the thread of enjoyment running through his voice making her want to kick him, hard. 'You too can bathe nude if you wish,' he added magnanimously.

'No, thank you.' Was he going to stand there and watch her undress? she asked herself desperately. It appeared that he was. 'I prefer to wear my bikini,' she said stiffly. 'And change in private.'

'As you like.' To her unutterable relief she heard him turn and move away from the car. 'I will wait for you in the water, *si*? But do not be too long or else I will have to come and fetch you.'

'Right.' Oh, help, oh, help, oh, help. . . Her mind was racing frantically as she quickly pulled off her jeans and pants behind the car door and slipped on the brief bikini bottom, before sitting on the back seat and fastening the clip to the minuscule bra, sliding the scrap of material over her breasts before taking off her top.

The ridiculousness of what she was doing, considering the fact that Donato had seen her naked more times than she could count, was not lost on her, but she was powerless to act differently. She felt more shy and vulnerable now than she ever had in their courting days or during the first intimacies of married life—more exposed and wide open to his virile brand of masculinity.

When she emerged from behind the car door, slamming it shut with a kind of childish bravado, the sweep of beach was deserted, Donato a mere speck in the glittering blue water. The sand was hot and powdery as she walked quickly to the water's edge, and, although the first shock of the water was cold on her overheated skin, once she had waded in to waist-depth she realised the water was actually beautifully warm.

She'd forgotten how good it was to swim in the sea. The thought stayed with her as she swam lazily through the small, curling waves, revelling in the silky coolness, only to gasp out loud and swallow a full mouthful of the salty water as Donato suddenly popped up beside her, grabbing her round the middle and laughing into her face. 'A mermaid in a black bikini,' he said softly.

Her shallow breathing and the flush that spread across her cheekbones was less to do with the residue of salt water, which tasted horrible, than the fact that the hard male body pressed against hers was hairy, sexy and very, very naked.

'Come on, I will race you to the big rock out there.' He inclined his head to a massive flat-topped protrusion some twenty-five yards away, against which gentle waves were lapping. 'First one there wins a prize.'

'Donato—'

But he had already pushed away, cutting through the water with powerful hard strokes before turning some few yards distant and flicking his head towards the rock. 'Come on—or do you want to ride piggy-back?' he called softly, wicked black eyes glittering.

He was already sitting on the sun-warmed stone when she reached it, his powerfully muscled body relaxed and dark with tiny droplets of water mingling with rough body hair like hundreds of tiny diamonds. 'You did not even try.' His voice was reproachful. 'But I still claim my prize.'

'Which is?' she asked warily, treading water slowly.

'This.' Before she could react he had leant across and pulled her up beside him, covering her body in one fluid movement so she lay beneath him. 'I have been wanting to do this too long.'

'Don't.' She struggled slightly but the smooth stone was hard beneath her outspread limbs and he was holding her too tightly for her wriggling to be effectual. 'I don't want this,' she said shakily.

'Liar.' He breathed the word deeply, slowly, like a caress, and she trembled at its sensuality. It was true; she was lying. And the knowledge was more frightening than anything else. 'You want me, Grace. We want each other—admit it,' he murmured huskily.

'I don't—' He cut off her voice by the simple expedient of lowering his mouth to hers, not in a harsh, dominating kind of kiss, but with a sweet stroking of her lips that combined with the powerful force of his hard body to become electrically erotic. He continued to move round her mouth in tiny featherlight kisses before his tongue moved where his lips had been, stroking, tasting, exploring, until the world was all light and colour behind her closed eyelids, her limbs relaxing on the warm, smooth stone.

When his hands wandered to her breasts they were

already ripe and throbbing, their tips hard and aroused from their contact with his rough body hair, and she shuddered as he peeled back the scrap of material to cup their swollen fullness before his head lowered to take what his hands had caressed. She gasped violently, she couldn't help it, her body arching as a piercing rush of sensation exploded through every nerve and sinew.

She heard him growl deep in his throat with pleasure at her primitive response, and then his mouth began a slow, languorous rhythmic assault on her silky skin that had her mindless beneath him, waves of sensation washing over her until she was moaning softly in her throat.

'Grace, Grace. . .' His mouth took hers again, hard and thrusting this time, the tremors that were shaking his body passing to hers, his arousal hot and fierce against her thighs. She wanted him, she needed him, oh, she did, so much. . . She loved him more than life itself—

The thought hit her at the same time as his hands moved to her bikini bottoms, and her reaction was instinctive—a violent push and jerk away that caught him completely by surprise, toppling him from both her and the smooth surface of the stone and straight into the cold deep blue water. She sat up in the same movement, fumbling with the bra top as she pulled it into place, her hands shaking so badly that she could hardly manipulate the damp material.

This was crazy, insane. Of course she didn't love him, she told herself feverishly. Not after what he'd done, the way he had betrayed her, let her walk out of his life without so much as a by your leave. She couldn't, she *couldn't* love a man like that. But she did. The knowledge was scalding and humiliating, and she dived off the rock and began to swim to shore as though her life depended on it.

He was beside her in the water almost at once, his strong, powerful strokes easily dominating her frantic splashing. 'Do I take it that was the equivalent of a cold shower?' He was angry—he was very angry, she realised with a sudden thudding of her heart as she noticed just how far away the shore was.

'I. . .I told you. I told you, didn't I, that I didn't want that?' She was barely coherent, her co-ordination going haywire as she swallowed another huge mouthful of salty seawater, causing her to choke and flounder, her arms and legs thrashing helplessly like a falling rag doll.

She felt his arms go round her and began to kick wildly, lashing out with her arms and legs as she lost all reason, governed purely by the feeling of panic and vulnerability that the self-knowledge of her love for him had exposed. He swore softly and savagely in his native tongue as he tried to subdue her, before using sheer brute force and turning her round, grasping her flailing body by the waist and towing her ignominiously to shore where he dumped her on the beach none too gently, his face black with rage.

'What the hell were you trying to do out there? Drown us both?' he snarled angrily. 'I was trying to help you, woman. Dammit, could you not see that?'

'I. . .I'm sorry.' She couldn't believe her actions in the last few minutes—what she had allowed in the way of lovemaking, her maniacal reaction as they had bordered on full intimacy and then her lunacy in the water when she could, as he had pointed out, have drowned them both.

'You are sorry.' He stood looking down at her like a dark avenging angel, fierce colour burning the high classical cheekbones and his black eyes bitter. 'What do you think I am, Grace? What do you *really* think I am? You thought I would take you by force in the water, is that it? In spite of the fact you had made your feelings very plain?'

'I didn't think that,' she whispered miserably, although she wasn't at all sure what she had thought, or whether she had been thinking at all.

'I do not believe you.' The formidable Vittoria pride had been severely dented, she could see that, but she thought she had glimpsed a desperate hurt in the blackness of his eyes before the ruthless mask he wore so well slid into place, hiding all emotion behind an expressionless façade. 'I think that is exactly what you thought, which is why you panicked so badly.' He held up an authoritative hand as she went to protest. 'Enough of this—are you hurt at all?'

'I. . .I don't think so.' She preferred the rage and fury he had shown at first to this icy, formal coldness.

'Then I suggest you change.' He had no idea how handsome he looked, she thought wretchedly, as he stood there stark naked, with a magnificent unconcern for his body that made him even more attractive. And she loved him, she loved him so much, and he was her husband, and the last few minutes had told her, without the shadow of a doubt, that she had to leave soon and never have contact with him again.

CHAPTER SIX

THE drive back to Alessandro and Anna's villa was an exercise in agony, the dinner that followed more so as Grace struggled to match Donato's polite, cool charm that revealed nothing of what had transpired between them. Nevertheless, she thought she saw Alessandro glance at his friend more than once with a keenness that told her he suspected something was badly amiss, although their Italian host was far too gracious to refer to it.

They left Amalfi just as it grew dark, the crescent moon shedding a thin, hollow light over the dark world below and the air warm and soft with the scents of summer in its languid stillness. Lorenzo curled up on the back seat and was asleep almost immediately, tired out after a day spent playing with his friend, which left Grace and Donato in a tense electric silence that crackled and buzzed with a tautness that was physically painful.

Don't cry, don't cry, don't cry. . . She spoke the warning to herself all the way back to Casa Pontina, staring out of the window with dry, burning eyes, vitally aware of the big lithe figure at her side. He must think she was crazy, mad, that she had lost it utterly, she thought with a stab of misery that closed her throat and made it hard to swallow. Either that or that she was the very worst sort of tease, delighting in taking him to the very edge of fulfilment before drawing away and saying no.

Not that she had actually said no, she thought miserably. No, she'd just pushed him straight off the rock into the sea like some outraged virgin defending an attack on her purity. It would be funny if it weren't so tragic. Oh. . . She screwed her eyes tightly shut in despair. What a mess she'd made of the day. She'd wanted to be clothed with cool dignity in all her dealings with him before she left Italy for good, and the time at the beach had resembled some sort of ridiculous farce.

'Do you wish to add cramp to your list of misfortunes?'

'What?' The dark, cool voice at her side made her nearly leap out of her seat as they drew into the slumbering grounds of Casa Pontina, so deeply had she been wrapped in her cloak of misery, and she checked herself angrily. She was like a cat on a hot tin roof round him, she thought painfully.

'I said, you will get cramp.' He gestured at her hands, so tightly clasped together that the knuckles were shining white through the flesh. 'Do you really consider me such a monster that you need be so afraid?' he asked softly, cutting the car engine as he spoke and turning to face her in his seat. 'I would not hurt you, Grace. It is clear you do not believe this, but it is true.'

But you have, you've hurt me so much there have been times I thought I'd die from it, she screamed silently. 'I'm not afraid of you, Donato.' She tried for a controlled flatness and blessed the result. 'It's just been a long day, that's all.'

'Grace——' His voice was urgent, fierce, but in the next instant Lorenzo had stirred in the back seat, sitting up and opening his eyes as he stretched noisily.

'Are we home?' the small boy asked sleepily. 'I have to see Benito, make sure he has been fed——'

'He will have been fed.' There was a wry note to Donato's voice now as he switched to big brother mode. 'Can you imagine Benito letting an important detail like that be overlooked? You will go straight to bed, Lorenzo, and that is an order. I will look in on Benito and make sure all is well.'

'All right.' Lorenzo was clearly too shattered to argue, and when Donato took his bulging bag from him made no protest. 'You will come and say goodnight?' he asked Grace now as they walked through the open front door into the house.

'In a minute.' She nodded and smiled but it was a

terrible effort. All she wanted to do was to run away and hide, dig a little hole somewhere and lie down and die. 'You get into your pyjamas and I'll be along once I've checked there are no messages for me,' she said reassuringly, giving him a little push towards the stairs.

'From whom?' Donato's voice was suddenly hard, almost suspicious. 'Are you expecting any calls?'

'Claire said she might ring.' She answered him mechanically, knowing she should tell him tonight of her intention to return to England as soon as she could book a flight, but fearful of her ability to remain calm and lucid. She felt like screaming, raging at him for the unfairness of the fact that she still loved him and he thought so little of her, so perhaps tonight was not a good time.

'Claire, I see.' She missed the lightening of his tone as she walked towards the door leading from the main house. There were no messages, but she used the interval to wash her face and comb her hair before she went back, feeling fractionally better for the quick freshening up as she knocked on Lorenzo's door.

'Come in.' It was Donato's deep voice that answered, causing her to hesitate a moment before she pushed the door open and stepped inside the dimly lit room. Lorenzo was snuggled down under his thin cotton quilt, looking impossibly angelic in red and blue Mickey Mouse pyjamas, and Donato straightened from smoothing the child's unruly hair from his forehead. 'He is nearly asleep,' he said softly.

'I am not.' But the weariness in the sleepy voice was a contradiction. 'I was staying awake until Grace came.'

'Goodnight, darling.' She had to force the words through numb lips. For a moment the similarity between this night and all those nights an eternity ago, when she and Donato would stand by Paolo's cot watching their baby drift off to sleep, was so poignant she felt ill. 'Sleep well,' she said gently.

The small boy was asleep before they had closed the bedroom door, and once outside on the dark landing she knew she had to escape quickly before the well of emotion that had been building all day overflowed. 'Goodnight.'

'Grace?' He caught her arm as she made to move away, turning her to face him, his eyes intent as they held hers. 'We have to talk. You know we have to talk?' he said urgently.

'I can't, not now.' If he didn't let go of her she was going to disgrace herself utterly for the second time that day, she knew it, she thought desperately. 'Tomorrow but not now.'

'Yes, now.' There was a note of steely determination in the implacable tones that she recognised of old. 'There are things that must be said: you cannot hide for ever.'

Hide? What was he talking about? she asked herself faintly.

'Do you want to talk downstairs in Bambina Pontina or in the room I am using?' he asked, swinging his hand to indicate the suite next to Lorenzo's. 'The choice is yours.'

Neither. She couldn't bear the thought of either of them. Their own home had too many memories, both poignant and distressing, and that afternoon had shown her the folly of being alone with him—especially in his bedroom. 'I'd rather leave this until tomorrow,' she said thickly, willing him to let her go.

'And I would not.' The tone was final.

She stared at him for a moment, sudden hot rage warring with the misery. He would not. That said it all, she thought bitterly. The great Donato Vittoria had spoken and must be obeyed. But she was too emotionally drained to argue any more. Suddenly it was all too much. 'The garden then.' She turned away, her mouth tremulous. 'If you insist on talking now I'd prefer to do it in the garden.'

'As you wish,' he said quietly, his voice calm and controlled.

As she wished? That was a joke, she thought desolately as they walked side by side down the curving staircase without touching. She *wished* this last two years had all been a terrible nightmare. She *wished* Paolo was still alive. She *wished* Donato hadn't found solace in another woman's arms. Oh—she wished so much and none of it could ever come true.

Self-pity. She was drowning in self-pity, she told herself with a touch of her old spirit as they reached Lorenzo's sitting room, continuing through to the paved area outside where Benito stirred slightly under the thick black sheet that covered his cage at night. But somehow those moments in his arms this afternoon and the revelation that she still loved him, despite telling herself the opposite for twelve long months, had weakened the tight guard she normally kept on her feelings.

They stepped off the patio, walking across a stretch of smooth lawn to where an old garden seat was enclosed in a semi-circle of flowers and tiny bushes that rose at the back of the small arbour in a brilliant display of colour: scarlet geraniums, lemon-scented verbenas, pink begonias, purple, red and white bougainvillea, all competing for supremacy in the perfumed air.

She had expected Donato to launch into some kind of verbal attack almost immediately, but he seemed content to sit quietly in the whispering stillness, the shadowed darkness lit slightly by the light of the moon and the lights from the house, the air warm and moist.

She would give the world to be able to turn back the clock, she thought with painful clarity. Anything, *everything* she possessed to return to the days when she was a happy, carefree wife and mother, content and satisfied with her husband and child. But she had changed. It was true what she had told Donato; she had changed irrevocably. The metamorphosis had begun with Paolo's death and perhaps wasn't complete even now.

'I can't believe I won't see his little face again,' she said quietly, her profile pure and delicate and her voice soft. 'I just want to hold him one more time, to tell him I love him, that I'm sorry I wasn't there when he needed me most.'

'Grace. . .' His voice was husky and he cleared his

throat before he began again, 'You have nothing to be sorry for, *mia piccola*. You heard the doctors; you know what they said. Nothing could have been done. It was one of those unexplained deaths that happens to hundreds, thousands of babies—'

'But he was *my* baby,' she said fiercely, turning to face him. 'I should have sensed something. I was his mother.'

'And I was his father.' The words were torn out of the depths of him. 'I was his father, Grace.'

'I know.' She turned her head, tears seeping out of her closed eyes. 'I know you loved him too. I know that, Donato.'

'Then why are you still punishing yourself and me for something that we could not have known would happen?' he asked gently. 'Do you not think that if there had been any sign, any hint of such a thing happening I would have moved heaven and earth to prevent it? You would have given your life for him, Grace, as would I. Do you not believe that?'

'But that doesn't bring him back.' The anguish was suddenly as piercing as in those first days, and Donato nodded slowly, his face sombre.

'No, it does not bring him back,' he agreed quietly, 'but this self-torture must end. It has to. You have scourged yourself to the limit, Grace, now there must come a day when we both start to live again.'

'I haven't stopped you living.' She stared at him, shocked and angry, the tears still trickling down her face. 'You know I haven't. How can you say something like that?'

'Because it is true.' His voice was firm and resolute, as though he had been waiting to tell her this for a long time. 'From the moment of his death it was true. You retreated from me, from our marriage—'

'*I* did? Oh, and you had nothing to do with it, I suppose?' she said with brittle control. 'It's all my fault, is that it?'

'For goodness' sake, woman, *listen* to me! I am not saying that—'

'Yes, you are.' She sprang up from the seat, her eyes hot and pain-filled. 'That's exactly what you are saying.'

'*Grace!*' Her name was bitten into the air, but even as she flinched against its sharpness he spoke again, the iron control back in place. 'Grace, sit down, please. Let us discuss this like adults.'

'I don't want to.' In a moment they were going to have an almighty row, it was quivering in the air like a live thing, and she didn't want that. She had left this marriage with nothing but her dignity and she was blowed if he was going to take that away from her, she thought wretchedly. 'I'm going in.'

'We have things to sort out,' he said tightly.

'We have nothing to sort out, Donato.' Her voice was cold now, but he wasn't to know it was the ice of desperation and panic that coated the pain beneath. He hadn't seen fit to give her even an explanation of his affair with Maria—no excuses, certainly no apologies. The great Donato Vittoria had acted and mustn't be questioned like ordinary mortals.

Well, so be it. She wasn't going to beg him to explain why he had acted as he had, and neither was she going to let him put all the blame on her. She hadn't been quite sane for a time after Paolo's death, she could accept that, but to take another woman into his bed. . .? 'We both made mistakes. Let's leave it like that. But it's finished— we're finished,' she said shakily, her control paper-thin.

'The hell we are.' His voice was a snarl now. 'So it goes on, the punishment? You didn't kill him, Grace. *I* didn't kill him—'

She couldn't listen to any more. She turned in one spinning movement and was halfway back to the house before he had the chance to react, skimming over the grass like a small pale ghost and not stopping in her headlong flight until she had safely locked the door of Bambina Pontina behind her. She slid the two bolts into place too, just in case he came after her and used the spare key that was kept in his study for emergencies, and then sank down on the tiles in front of the door as her trembling legs refused to hold her any longer.

She hated him—hated him and loved him and wanted him. . . Her tears were hot and acidic and she cried until there were none left and she lay shuddering on the floor, spent and exhausted.

Paolo. The angry exchange in the garden had opened old wounds she thought had healed but now realised were as raw as the day her baby had died. She continued to lie there for more than an hour, and gradually, as she accepted that Donato wasn't going to come after her and the night enveloped her in its warm, dark serenity, she faced the truth in Donato's words.

Part of her withdrawal from Donato and from life itself after their baby's death had been due to shock and grief, but underlining it all had been guilt that she and Donato had been together, laughing, talking, making love—her stomach clenched and she shut her eyes tightly, her face screwed up as though she had a physical pain—while their child had died. She hadn't been able to accept that part of the tragedy.

She sat up abruptly, hugging her knees as she stared blindly ahead, searching her feelings slowly and tentatively. She *had* been punishing them both, she thought painfully, without realising it and without any logic. She had felt they had to pay, that they had no right to be alive when they had let their baby die. *But it hadn't been their fault—her fault.*

'It wasn't anyone's fault,' she breathed softly into the quiet of the night as something lifted that had been holding her captive for long months and her heart finally accepted what her brain had known all along. It was true. She and Donato would both have given their lives for their son without a moment's hesitation. They just hadn't had the chance, because life didn't come in neatly wrapped little packages where A equalled B, and everything was fair and even-handed.

She pulled herself up from the floor and walked

through to the kitchen, making herself a cup of coffee before taking it up to her room and padding out onto the balcony in the cool of the night, lifting her face to the soft, perfumed air.

Love, such a complex emotion. She sipped the hot drink, her thoughts ranging to and fro. She had never fully accepted that Donato loved her, that this handsome, wealthy, powerful man who could have any woman he wanted had chosen her.

She remembered the words he had spoken to her on her wedding day, when he had touched the huge bouquet of wild flowers in her trembling hands. 'I wanted this day to be perfect for you. I want all the days from here on to be perfect for you, *mia piccola*. Do you understand this? All the fears of your heart, all the dark memories, all the times when you have been alone and had no one to share with, these can now all be given to me and I will make it right. There is nothing you can ever tell me, no matter how big or small, that I will not listen to. I love you, my delicate little English rose. I will always love you, and in time I will teach you to love yourself.'

But she had never learned. She sat bolt-upright now, the hot coffee splashing over her hand although she didn't feel it. Even when Paolo was born and life had been so perfect it had frightened her. She was still the shy, nervous little girl from the children's home who was never chosen by prospective adoptive parents because she wasn't bright or confident or sparkling enough. Her adult skin had merely hidden the insecure uncertain child within; she had always been waiting for a time when she would do something to spoil the dream she was living in.

As though it was yesterday the memories came rushing in, hot and fast. She had been at the children's home six months when the Blairs had begun to take her out for the odd day, and had still been missing her mother and father desperately as well as having to adjust to school life and life in the home.

Charles and Caroline Blair had been the original yuppies, she supposed now with hindsight, but the handsome, distinguished-looking man and his elegant, beautiful wife had mesmerised her with their magnificent home and string of cars. She had tried so hard to please them, saying and doing the right thing when they had shown her off like a little doll to their sophisticated friends.

After a few visits the Blairs had arranged to have her live with them for a week or so—'a little holiday', the matron at the home had termed it, although she had known even then that she was being considered for adoption—and things had gone well—for the first two days. And then on the third night she had had a bad dream, one that had recurred on and off since the trauma of her parents' death, and had woken crying and screaming in her luxurious bedroom of pink and white.

Charles and Caroline had come to her, the former annoyed and irritated and the latter daintily displeased at the sight of her wet blotchy face and anguished sobs, and their combined distaste had left her wide-eyed and hiccuping through the rest of the long, dark night. Not that they had been physically unkind to her, she thought now, not at all, but she had sensed something in their eyes that had told her she'd misbehaved in some way.

She had been dispatched back to the home at the end of the week with no promises of further visits, and the episode might not have left such permanent damage if she hadn't overheard a conversation between Caroline Blair and the matron of the home the day after her return.

She had been sent along to the matron's office with a request for something—she couldn't remember what now—and had been just on the point of knocking when she had heard Caroline's voice from within. 'I'm sorry, Mrs Jennings, but I'm afraid it just didn't work out as we expected.' There had been a slight pause and then, 'We had no idea Grace was such a. . .fierce little thing.'

'Grace?' Matron's voice was frankly disbelieving. 'You're telling me you found Grace difficult? In what way, Mrs Blair? I shall need you to be specific.'

'So terribly emotional and excitable. . .' There followed the light, tinkling little laugh that Caroline Blair used so well, and the sound of it gnawed at Grace's stomach as she stood there, hardly daring to breathe. 'Really, Mrs Jennings, she just wasn't what we had thought initially. I don't know quite how to explain it.'

'Try.' The tone of the Matron's voice suggested to Grace that she was angry, and Caroline Blair must have picked that up too, because when she next spoke her voice was conciliatory, with a faint touch of defensiveness about it.

'Perhaps all the aggravation was as much our fault as Grace's,' she said in honeyed tones. 'I remember at the start of our interviews you mentioned it isn't every couple who can successfully take on someone else's child once they are older. But Grace seemed to fit in so well on her earlier visits. She was so appreciative of all we could give her—'

'And you expected gratitude, Mrs Blair, and Grace wasn't sufficiently humble? Did she offend you in some way?' the matron asked intuitively, her voice carefully expressionless.

'Well, she still seems to want her parents,' Caroline Blair said, in a tone that expressed her amazement at the fact.

'What did you expect? Grace was an only child who lost both her parents in a car accident and had her life changed overnight. You are aware of all the facts. It takes time for children to come to terms with such a tragedy,' Matron said coldly.

'Yes, but she always appeared so sweet and quiet, such a pretty little thing—'

Again there had been a pause and now, looking back down the years with adult eyes, Grace could just imagine Matron's face as she had viewed the other woman, she so thick and stout and down to earth and the other possessed of an ethereal gracefulness that had verged on languidness.

'I thought she understood all we could do for her, that she would be far better off with us than. . .'

'Her own parents? This is all about her missing her own parents? Mrs Blair, at the risk of sounding impertinent, might I suggest that a pet poodle would suit your lifestyle better than a child?' Matron's voice was acidic.

'Well, really—!'

'And I feel it only fair to warn you that I shall be writing to Social Services to inform them of what has taken place here today, and to say that I do not consider you and your husband suitable parents for one of my children,' Matron continued coldly.

'How dare you? How *dare* you?' There was nothing languid about Caroline Blair's voice now, and she fairly spat at the older woman. 'My husband and I are leading lights in our community, I would have you know. We can offer a child everything—*everything*. Just because I object to your presenting me with a child who is clearly unsuitable—'

'That is not it at all, Mrs Blair, and you know it,' Matron said stoically. 'In the first place you seemed to take to Grace initially, and she to you, and in the second it is the underlying thread in this report you have given me—' there was the sound of paper rustling, as though it had been flicked by an angry hand '—that is a cause for concern. In spite of the procedure you have undergone, I don't think you and your husband appreciate what is involved in taking on a child. If I may speak plainly, a child is more than a social appendage or a reflection on your status. Children are flesh and blood human beings, with hurts and needs and desires.'

There was more, much more, but after a minute or two Grace moved away from the door, her small face white and stricken and her body shaking with reaction at what she had heard. Her young mind absorbed the fact that she wasn't wanted because she had failed in some way, that she was to blame for the conversation behind the closed door, and it was that which stayed with her through her childhood and adolescence, colouring her view of herself so deeply that she became quiet and withdrawn and introverted, always hanging back behind the other children when she could, and rarely venturing an opinion about anything.

So it had seemed all the more miraculous when, on her first venture into the outside world, Donato had blazed onto her horizon and encompassed her in his fire, transporting her into a life of love and laughter and freedom. Until Paolo had died.

Grace winced, shaking her head at her thoughts. Then the five-year-old child had re-emerged from the woman's body, telling her it was her fault, that she wasn't good enough, worthy enough to deserve her husband and child, that she had let Paolo die.

'But I didn't.' She spoke out loud, her voice tinged with wonder at the enormity of her liberation as the chains and fetters of years fell from her. 'It wasn't my fault—our fault. . .'

Donato had known, even in those early days he had known she blamed herself, and he had talked to her endlessly, trying to force logic past the devastating emotion that held her in its black grip. But she had rejected his help then—that had been part of her punishment, she thought shakily. And after the night of her birthday party he had stopped trying.

She sat quietly on the cool balcony through the dark night hours, slowly coming to terms with the past, and although she must have dozed once or twice she was awake when a pink-tipped dawn crept over the velvety blackness heralding the new day.

She wasn't sure if she heard Donato first or sensed him in the grounds below the window, but a shadowy twilight was still hanging in the early-morning air when the tall, dark shape became visible to her tired eyes.

She instinctively edged back but he seemed quite unaware of her presence above, clearly lost in thoughts of his own, moving quietly among the shadows until he was lost from sight in the vast gardens. She continued to stare into the soft twilight that was becoming clearer by the moment for some minutes, before sagging back in her chair, her hand to her mouth, biting the base of her thumb as anguish pierced her soul.

She loved him. She loved him so much. But in the final analysis sex had been more important to him than she was. It had only been six months from Paolo's death to her twenty-first birthday, and that had been the first time he had taken Maria.

She could tell herself he'd had mitigating circumstances, that he too had been suffering and had needed bodily comfort after his son's death, that men could use a woman for sexual release and it didn't mean anything to them—oh, a hundred and one excuses. But he had given someone else the rights only she should have had, had kissed her, touched her, joined his body to hers. . . 'I can't bear it, I can't,' she whispered brokenly as hot tears scalded her vision.

She closed her eyes tightly, rocking back and forth in her seat and whimpering deep in her throat. It wasn't even that she hadn't forgiven him, she thought torturously. Perhaps he, too, hadn't been thinking straight, had been closed in with his grief, but that still didn't get rid of the pictures in her mind and it never would.

She could forgive him but she could never live with him again, not being the sort of woman she was. Another person might manage it, but not her. It wouldn't be fair to either of them to pretend differently. And she couldn't stay any longer in Italy; she had to leave *now*.

She opened her eyes, staring blindly ahead. She would leave today, and if he thought she was running away again. . .so be it.

CHAPTER SEVEN

IT WAS a time-worn phrase of Mrs Jennings' that came to mind some hours later when Grace went downstairs to breakfast, only to find her decision turned upside down as soon as she stepped into the breakfast room. 'The best laid plans of mice and men only come to nought'. She had heard the stout matron speak it on numerous occasions throughout her childhood, but it had never seemed so apt as now.

'The *signore*, he wants you upstairs.' Gina had clearly been waiting for her, dark eyes anxious. 'It is Lorenzo, he has the ache in the head, and here. . .' The maid's hands fluttered agitatedly near her throat.

'Lorenzo has a sore throat and headache?' Grace paused just inside the room, glancing back towards the stairs. 'When did this start, Gina? Has he been ill in the night?'

'I do not know, *signora*, but the *signore*, he is worried. Lorenzo, he has the fever, *sì*? He very hot, *signora*.'

'Has the doctor been called?' Grace asked over her shoulder as she turned and hurried towards the stairs.

'*Sì, sì, signora*, at once, at once,' Gina called after her.

When Grace reached Lorenzo's room she entered immediately after a perfunctory knock to discover the small boy tossing and turning in a rumpled bed and Donato trying to bathe his brother's hot head with cool water, his dark face grim and set.

'He did not call me until a few minutes ago but he has been like this for some time.' Donato's voice was agitated and tense, and so unlike the normal cool, lazy tones she was used to that she found herself staring at him in surprise as she joined him at Lorenzo's bedside. However, she saw at once that Donato was right to be

121

concerned. The child was clearly burning up with a high temperature and mumbling deliriously, his eyelids flickering.

'Run a tepid bath, Donato,' she said quietly, trying to keep all obvious alarm from her voice. 'Quickly.'

'A bath?' He glanced at her as though she was mad. 'He needs a doctor, not a bath.'

'I know that, but until the doctor arrives we need to try and lower his temperature.' She pulled the light cotton quilt off Lorenzo as she spoke, before taking off the jacket of his pyjamas and sponging water over his torso and arms from the bowl on the bedside cabinet, trying not to panic at the heat emanating from the small frame.

Once the shallow bath was ready Donato carried the limp body of his brother through to the bathroom, and, after stripping the covers, Grace remade his bed with fresh linen and switched on the large fan in one corner of the room to cool the air.

By the time Donato carried Lorenzo back into the bedroom the air temperature was a few degrees lower, and it was clear that the cool water had helped because the small boy was lucid again. 'My head hurts.' He stared up at Grace from the bed, his brown eyes enormous in his flushed cheeks. 'And I cannot swallow.'

'You can swallow, although it hurts.' She smiled as she spoke, trying to maintain a calm, matter-of-fact approach when in reality she was longing for the doctor as much as Donato, who had stridden to the window growling impatiently under his breath. 'If I ask Gina to bring you a drink with something in it to make you feel better, will you try to drink it?' she asked quietly.

'*Sì.*' But as she made to move away from the bed he spoke again, his voice panic-stricken. 'I do not want you to go, Grace. Stay here.' He lifted thin arms towards her, his eyes filling with tears.

'I will see to it.' Donato swung round abruptly. 'You are thinking of junior paracetamol?' he asked gruffly.

'Yes.' Their eyes met for a moment and she felt her heart leap and begin to thud at the look on his face. He hadn't shaved—obviously Lorenzo had called him before his normal ablutions were completed—and the devastatingly attractive stubble combined with his tousled hair and air of worried uncertainty was incredibly seductive, combining as it did man and boy. He was dynamite. She pulled her eyes from his with an effort that made her dizzy. He always had been and always would be, and she was going to go stark staring mad before all this was finished.

The doctor arrived just as Donato returned with the orange drink and his diagnosis was immediate. 'Scarlet fever.' He nodded at them both as they hovered by the bed. 'Half the children in this area are down with it; it is a highly infectious disease. I can already see the slight beginnings of the rash on his chest—it will spread over the whole body soon.'

'Is it dangerous?' Grace asked quietly after the doctor had indicated for Donato to go ahead and give Lorenzo the drink.

'Not these days.' It was the same doctor who had come to the house the day Paolo died. He had been the Vittoria family doctor for years, and he smiled gently now, his voice encouraging as he patted Grace's hand. 'Before antibiotics the story was quite different, but now scarlet fever can be rapidly cured with penicillin. Please do not distress yourself.

'The fever is the main concern—the sore throat and headache will diminish of their own accord. But it is important to keep him cool while the rash is developing. He will be somewhat fractious, of course. The Vittoria males do not like to be anything but one hundred per cent fit, do they?' His voice was wry as he spoke the last words but not unkind.

'No.' She smiled back, remembering how kind he had been to her in the black weeks following their loss, often calling at the house unannounced just to see how she was and spending valuable time merely talking to her, never betraying, by word or action, that his time was precious and he had a hundred and one other patients to see to.

He gave Lorenzo an antibiotic injection before he went downstairs, leaving further medication with Donato, who returned immediately to the room after seeing the doctor out. 'How is he?' The question was superfluous, and so unlike Donato's normal hard, formidable and totally logical attitude in a crisis that again she found herself staring at him before tearing her eyes away from his disturbingly attractive face.

'Exactly the same as when you left two minutes ago,' she replied lightly, 'and stop worrying. You heard what the doctor said—he'll be fine. We just need to keep his temperature down for the next little while. Now go and get something to eat. We'll be all right.'

The next forty-eight hours were exhausting rather than traumatic and at the end of them Lorenzo resembled a well boiled lobster, the red rash almost covering his body, but thankfully his temperature was down and already he was fretting to go downstairs and see Benito, which Grace took as a good sign. However, the Vittoria obstinacy was a force to be reckoned with, and she was in the middle of explaining, for the hundredth time, why Lorenzo couldn't venture downstairs that day when Donato's deep voice from the doorway cut into her patient exposition.

'I do not expect Grace to have to explain to you again, Lorenzo.' There was a very definite warning in the dark tones. 'You are still most unwell—you were barely able to visit the bathroom by yourself this morning—and you will do as you are told.'

It had slowly dawned on Grace over the last day or so that Donato's relationship with his brother was more that of a father with a child than anything else, a fact that had not been so obvious when their mother was alive mainly due to the fact that Lorenzo had spent most of his time with Liliana. Their father had died when Lorenzo was just five, so Donato's natural acceptance of the role as father-figure to his small brother was not surprising when she thought about it, but the reality hadn't hit her until Lorenzo had become ill and she had seen the extent of Donato's love for his small charge.

The knowledge increased her respect for him as well as deepening the tender affection that was quite a separate feeling from her love, and she knew both emotions were dangerous and weakening.

'But, Donato, he will be wondering where I am.' Lorenzo turned soulful eyes up to Grace. 'He is my friend,' he added mournfully. 'My best friend.'

'And I am your brother,' Donato said, with a touch of amusement colouring his voice, 'and I do not have Grace's soft heart, so you need not try your wiles on me, Lorenzo. The doctor said a few days in bed and a few days in bed is what you will have. Benito is an intelligent bird, as well you know, and I am sure he will bear the separation with great fortitude.'

It was said tongue in cheek, and Lorenzo glanced at his brother from under his thick black eyelashes before suddenly deciding this was one battle he couldn't win and grinning whimsically.

'Can I have my games console up here, then?' he asked hopefully. 'I haven't tried the new games Giuseppe lent me yet.'

'You may, as long as you play for a short time and sleep this afternoon—and no more trying to twist Grace's arm.'

He handled the child well—very well, Grace thought as she left Lorenzo watching television and followed Donato out of the room in obedience to the slight inclination of his head. Just the right amount of firmness combined with love. He had been an excellent father too, gentle and loving and quite prepared to enter into every aspect of caring for his tiny son.

She remembered the shock on Liliana's face when she had caught him changing Paolo's nappy one day, Donato's father having been of the old school who considered such necessities strictly women's work, and found herself smiling at the memory.

'That is better.' As Donato's hand traced a path across her cheek to the smooth curve of her mouth she felt his touch in every part of her body, its heat melting her limbs and turning her bones liquid. 'It is good to see you smile.' His dark eyes moved to the pure line of her throat, where a tiny pulse was beating frantically, and as his hand moved down the slender length of her neck she began to tremble, quite unable to hide what his nearness was doing to her. '*Bella, bella*,' he murmured softly. 'Your skin is like silk.'

'Donato, don't. . . I . . . Please—'

'Shh, *mia piccola*.' He eased her into the hard line of his body, one hand in the small of her back as the other lifted her chin to meet his gaze. 'We talk too much, that is the problem. 'Your body melts to my touch as mine does for you. It has always been so.'

'No!' She gasped the protest but he caught it with his mouth, his lips fiercely possessive as they took hers.

She tried to pull away but he was holding her too tightly, his mouth urgent and demanding as he moved her round, still locked in his embrace, until she was standing with her back to the wall held captive by his body. He slid his hands down to the swell of her hips, moving her against him in such a way that she could feel every inch of his arousal and the pounding of his heart as it slammed against his ribcage.

'I want you, my sweet, beautiful little English wife,' he murmured thickly. 'I want you so badly I can taste it. I have dreamed of touching you like this so many long, empty nights, when the smell and feel of you was all around me, sending me mad. You are part of me, Grace, you are in my blood.'

He devoured her mouth, the raging need that had taken control of him spinning her into a sweet, potent experience that was all sensation. Their breathing was ragged, desperate, their bodies locked together as though in the very act of possession, straining against each other as they swayed in an age-old rhythm of passion.

'Come into my room. . .' It was a few seconds before

his words registered, and by then he had moved them
both across the landing, his hand already on the door-
handle before reason returned.

'I can't, Donato, I can't.' She jerked backwards, her
eyes wild. 'I haven't lied to you. I've told you all along
that I intend to go home—'

'This is your home,' he said softly. 'This will always
be your home. You belong here, Grace, with me.'

'No.' It was easier now he wasn't touching her, and
still more so when his face hardened and became cold.
'That morning Lorenzo was ill, I'd intended to tell you
then I was ready to leave.' Her voice was quivering,
weak, and she hated herself for it.

'But I am not ready to let you go,' he said arrogantly,
his big, muscular body held taut and straight. 'Perhaps
I will never be ready.' He eyed her challengingly, all
softness gone.

'Then that's your problem, not mine.' His insolent
hauteur was the final douche of cold water that extingu-
ished the flames of desire and she was desperately
grateful for it. Donato Vittoria, lord of the manor, she
could fight, but that other Donato, the one who brought
a thousand sweet, disturbing memories to life. . .

'Be careful, *mia piccola*.' He didn't move so much as
a muscle, but she was suddenly vitally conscious of the
ruthless side of him and it sent a shiver flickering down
her spine. 'Be very careful. I will only allow so much.'

'Perhaps I don't care what you will allow any more.
Have you considered that?' she asked tightly. 'I've made
a new life for myself—I'm a person in my own right
now, not just an appendage to you.'

'Now you are being ridiculous,' he snarled angrily,
'absurd! When the hell were you ever made to feel
like that?'

'Donato. . .' She paused, taking a deep breath and
forcing herself to speak calmly, flatly. She would
never win a war of words with that rapier-sharp tongue
and she didn't intend to try. The facts spoke for themselves and it was the facts she had to cling on to—not

her emotions, not her weakness, and certainly not her love for him. He had started an affair with a girl who had always made it plain she was ready and willing. He had used Maria and he had used her.

He had let her walk out of his life and then called her back, like a little puppy-dog to heel, when he required her to fulfil a need in Lorenzo's life. Those were the facts. *Those were the facts.* 'I shall leave once Lorenzo is well again,' she said stiffly, forcing the words through numb lips, 'and I shan't come back. Lorenzo can visit me in England if you want him to, stay with me for the holidays—'

'How very gracious,' he said coldly.

'But I am going to go.' She stared at him for one long moment, waiting for shouting, an outburst, a reaction of some kind, but he merely returned her gaze, his eyes as cold as ice, until she lowered her head and walked past him and along the landing on shaking legs, reaching the top of the stairs and descending slowly as she held tightly to the beautifully carved rail with every step, feeling as though her legs were going to give way at any moment.

It was over. She might not leave for another week or two but it was over. She had read it in the blankness of his eyes. So why, when she knew it had to be this way, did she feel as though the world were coming to an end?

The next few days were ones of subtle torment for Grace. It wasn't so bad when Lorenzo was still ensconced upstairs, although she was on tenterhooks constantly, expecting every knock at Lorenzo's bedroom door to herald Donato's appearance. But after the second day, when Lorenzo was well enough to move downstairs to his sitting room and to Benito for most of the time, she realised Donato was avoiding her and it hurt.

Stupid, illogical, unreasonable, were just a few of the words she threw at herself, but nevertheless a sick misery had taken her over, and the nervous energy she used each day in hiding her distress from Lorenzo and being bright and cheerful was making her feel ill.

The penicillin had successfully taken care of any possible side effects of the illness which had proved so disabling in the past, and when Bianca called by to see Lorenzo, a week after he had first become ill, the small boy was virtually back to normal—which for some reason seemed to grate unbearably with his sister.

'Lorenzo? What is this?' The Italian woman stood in the doorway to the sitting room, manicured hands on slender hips and eyes slanted in disapproval as she took in the huge Lego fort Grace and Lorenzo had been busy building for most of the day. 'You are ill, no? This is not a time for excitement. Why are you not in bed?'

'I was in bed,' Lorenzo said indignantly, his small face wearing the habitual look of defensiveness that any contact with his sister caused. 'But I am much better now.'

'Hmph!' Bianca gave one of the sarcastic sighs she was so good at. 'You are a child; you do not know what is best. Why did you allow him to get up so quickly?' she added without pausing for breath, her words directed at Grace now as her eyes narrowed still more. 'You do not care if he becomes ill again?'

'Of course I care, but Lorenzo is fine,' Grace said quietly, and she warned herself not to bite back. It was clear that for some reason Bianca was looking for a fight, and the last thing Lorenzo needed was any unpleasantness. The child had missed his mother badly during the worst of his illness, but Grace had devoted herself to keeping him as cheerful as possible and her hard work seemed to have paid off—that and the presence of the irascible Benito, who could always be relied on to provide entertainment.

'And you think you are a good judge of whether a child is fine?' It was a direct punch below the belt, and for a moment Grace couldn't believe Bianca had actually said what she had with such premeditated cruelty, but the venomous spite in her face was confirmation.

Both women knew Bianca was referring to Paolo's death, but Grace forced herself to play down the incident.

'Yes, I think so. Most women are.' She knew Bianca's tactics of old, and there was no way she was going to jump in and fire back so that matters escalated into a full-scale row in front of Lorenzo.

'That is rubbish.' Bianca sauntered more fully into the room, her slim body encased in tight blue jeans and a white silk shirt and her long, silky black hair held in a French plait which accentuated her wonderful cheekbones. She looked beautiful—beautiful and confident and very, very cruel, like a glossy black cat enjoying itself playing with a captive bird. 'You have had no medical training, I think?' she asked smoothly.

'One hardly needs medical expertise to deal with scarlet fever,' Grace said shortly, 'or mothers all over the world would be in difficulty.'

'But you are not Lorenzo's mother.' The words were snapped into the air with unmistakable venom. 'In fact you are not even Italian! You are nothing to him.'

'She is!' Lorenzo was scarlet with outrage as he leapt to his Grace's defence, both verbally and physically, jumping to his feet as he faced Bianca, his thin hands clenched into fists at his side. 'She is and she loves me,' he said fiercely.

'Control yourself.' The words were bitten out through clenched teeth, and in that moment no one could have called Bianca beautiful.

'No, I will not! You are not to say bad things about Grace. I will not allow it, do you hear? She is. . .she is. . .'

'*Sì*? What exactly is your wonderful Grace?' Bianca asked, with a mocking cruelty that was none the less effective for being forced. It was clear the Italian woman would have liked to grab hold of her brother and use physical force to subdue him, and just as obvious that she didn't dare go quite that far.

'She is my second mother.' Lorenzo brought out the words with the air of one who had just discovered something momentous. 'And I love her,' he added for good measure as Bianca's face blazed.

There followed a torrent of Italian between brother

and sister which Grace wouldn't have been able to follow even if Lorenzo's words hadn't sent her into a state of panic and alarm. She had known the child loved her, as she did him, but the depth of his love was deeper than she had ever imagined.

The words hadn't been said lightly, in fact they had been torn out of him, and Grace knew he would never have voiced his feelings if Bianca hadn't forced the issue. But now he had spoken it was going to make her leaving a thousand times worse. But she couldn't stay. There was only one way she could live for any length of time at Casa Pontina and that would be on Donato's terms—she knew him well enough to know that—and even if he could be persuaded to let her live a separate existence from him the situation would be impossible. Her love for him, if nothing else, would see to that.

'What is going on here?' The words were like pistol-shots, and the deep, angry voice from the doorway silenced Bianca and Lorenzo's frenzied exchange in much the same way a bullet would have done. 'Well?' Donato's voice held all the softness of finely honed steel, slicing through the air as his glittering eyes took in the scene in front of him. 'Who is going to explain?'

'It is Lorenzo, he is *so* bad—unruly.' Bianca recovered almost immediately, her lovely face taking on an aggrieved expression that would have convinced Grace the Italian woman was the injured party if she had not known differently. 'He says that Grace is his mother, that I am nothing to him.'

'I did not!' Lorenzo's protest was loud and tearful, and Grace put her arms round the small boy as she added her voice to his, glaring at Bianca angrily as she did so.

'He did not say that Bianca is nothing to him—'

'Enough! We will discuss this when everyone is calmer,' Donato said sternly. 'And as for you two. . .' He turned furious eyes on his siblings. 'I could hear you from the drive. How dare you bring the Vittoria name into disrepute by behaving like gutter children? If I had had someone with me—'

'But you didn't.' The mention of the Vittoria name was the last straw for Grace, and it was only Lorenzo's thin little body pressed close to hers that stopped her from yelling herself. The wonderful, marvellous Vittoria name! Was that the only thing that mattered to him? Of course it was—why ask when she already knew?

'No, I did not.' The glance Donato bestowed on her would have crushed lesser mortals, but she was too angry, and too concerned for Lorenzo to care. 'Now, shall we retire to the drawing room and discuss the matter in a civilised fashion?' he said icily.

'Oh, Donato. . .' Bianca's eyes were liquid, and Grace wasn't surprised to see the other woman squeeze out a tear as she took her older brother's arm, her small hand fragile against his bulk. 'I cannot understand why he hates me so, I am so upset. . .'

'You are also old enough to know better.' Donato's voice was cold but Grace noticed he didn't remove Bianca's arm from his, and as Donato and Bianca led the way out of the room Bianca turned and gave the other two a crocodile smile of satisfaction.

She's evil. Grace felt a shiver snake down her spine and she hugged Lorenzo swiftly before they followed, dreading the coming confrontation.

Thank goodness Benito hadn't been in the room. The parrot would certainly have added to the melee, and she dreaded to think what he would have said! Fortunately, Anna and Gina had taken his cage and perch to the kitchens for their daily scrub just before Bianca arrived, a little part of the day's routine Benito always enjoyed due to the fact the maids, ever mindful of the lethal beak and claws, plied him with all his favourite titbits to keep him co-operative.

From the way Donato had spoken Grace had expected an immediate and ruthless interrogation once they were seated, but, after pulling the cord to summon one of the maids, Donato gestured at Lorenzo, still held protectively in the curve of Grace's arm on the sofa. 'You are calm now?' he asked quietly, his voice cool.

'*Si.*' Lorenzo clearly felt ill done by on the one hand, but the Vittoria male in him also acknowledged his lack of control as reprehensible. The conflict was there to see in the small, thin face in which the huge liquid eyes provided a window into his soul, and Grace thought she saw Donato's lips twitch just the slightest bit as he surveyed his young brother through expressionless eyes.

'Then I think that after apologising to me for your lapse it would be a good idea to have your bath early with a tea-tray in bed? It is not so many days ago that you were very ill.'

'Is that all you are going to say——?'

He cut short Bianca's sharp protest with one narrowed glance before turning to Lorenzo again. 'Well?' he asked steadily.

'I am sorry, Donato, for shouting,' Lorenzo said with a stoic determination to make it clear that that was all he was sorry for. 'I will not do it again, I promise you.'

'Good.' Donato nodded his acceptance of the apology and then, as Anna came into the room, continued, 'Anna, will you arrange a tea-tray for Lorenzo in his room in thirty minutes? And would you inform Cecilia the *signora* and I are eating out tonight?'

'*Sì, signore.*' Anna glanced at the unsmiling faces and left quickly.

'Donato?' Once Anna had left the room Lorenzo spoke quickly, while Grace was still deciding if she had heard what she thought she had heard. She wasn't going to eat out with Donato. She wasn't going to do *anything* with Donato! 'May I say goodnight to Benito before I go upstairs?' he asked pleadingly. 'Please?'

'That horrible creature!' I would not be surprised if it is the bird that has made Lorenzo ill,' Bianca said with a theatrical little shiver and a spiteful glance at Lorenzo. 'They are full of germs.'

'I am sure there are many crimes that can be laid at Benito's feet, but passing on scarlet fever is not one of them.' Donato's cool voice overrode the hot protest from Lorenzo, and then he added, 'You may have five minutes with Benito—okay?—and then your bath. You must not tire yourself at this stage of your recovery and I want you settling down for sleep in one hour.'

Lorenzo scuttled out of the room without further conflict with his sister, contenting himself with directing one angry glance at Bianca before he left, the lethal content of which expressed all he couldn't say and more. If Donato noticed the exchange he didn't comment on it.

'Really, Donato, you are too lenient with the child. He is becoming obnoxious,' Bianca said vindictively. 'I am ashamed of him.'

'Enough, Bianca.' If Donato's voice had been cold before, now it was positively glacial. 'I will deal with Lorenzo as I see fit, but suffice it to say if you were still living under my roof I would have made sure this house was not subject to the kind of behaviour you indulged in earlier.'

'But what was I supposed to do when he began shouting?' Bianca whined sulkily.

'Lorenzo is ten years old and has recently passed through the worst sort of trauma a child can experience. To say that your attitude regarding him lacks sensitivity is putting it mildly.'

'I'll go and make sure Lorenzo is getting ready for bed.' Grace fled the scene on winged feet, but although Donato acknowledged her departure with a curt nod of his head she didn't think Bianca was even aware of her going, her almond eyes fixed on her brother's face and her cheeks scarlet with outrage at being taken to task.

It was some time later when Donato joined her in Lorenzo's sitting room, where she was busy tidying away the small boy's toys. As she became aware of a presence she swung round nervously to find him regarding her from the doorway, his dark eyes intent on her face. 'I see Lorenzo is taking advantage of your good nature,' he said wryly. 'He is quite able to take care of all that himself, you know. You are not his nursemaid.'

'I know, and he would have tidied up, but I said I'd do it. He was tired.' Her face and her voice were defensive. 'I like. . .I like looking after him,' she added uncomfortably.

'And yet you are intent on leaving him soon. You know he will be devastated?' Donato asked softly, walking fully into the room and crouching down beside her as she packed Lego bricks into a large plastic box. 'He was inconsolable until you came.'

'That's not fair, Donato.' Neither was the way his trousers had pulled tight across his thighs, accentuating hard-muscled flesh.

'You ask me to be fair, *mia piccola*?' he murmured huskily. 'You ask too much. I am not made of stone.'

'It's seemed like it the last few days,' she bit back without thinking, her mind trying to cope with the overwhelming effect his nearness was having on her senses. But immediately the words had left her lips she regretted them. They revealed too much.

'Ah. . .you are piqued I have not begged for your attention?' he asked softly. 'But that is not my way—you know this. I will only take what is freely given.'

'I'm not piqued, I don't want. . .I don't need. . .' She stumbled to a halt, mesmerised by the delicious smell and feel of him as his mouth opened over hers in a kiss that was all-consuming, his lips and tongue plundering the softness within.

He had always been able to make her melt with his kisses, she thought tremblingly as her mind spun and dipped. From the very first evening she had met him, when he had engineered to get her alone in the kitchen of his friend's home, she had known she would never meet another man who could kiss like him.

'What *do* you want, Grace? What *do* you need?' he asked thickly after raising his head to look into her flushed face, his eyes dark and glittering. 'For me to love you until the flames consume us both? To be naked in my arms so I can touch you, kiss you, taste you all over? Because that is what I want. Do you know what you do to me? Do you? With your pale, soft English skin and your hair of fire? I want you, *mia piccola*, never doubt that. I have always wanted you.'

'But wanting is not enough,' she whispered painfully. 'There has to be more.' Like commitment, whatever the difficulties. Trust, whatever the temptation. Faithfulness. . .

He stared at her for one moment more and then stood up slowly, pulling her with him and holding her against him. 'I have reserved a table at Rinaldi's tonight for eight o'clock,' he said quietly, his eyes dark and veiled. 'Please be ready.'

'I don't think—'

'I am not asking you to think,' he said softly, 'I am asking you to be ready for an evening out with me. You say you intend to leave soon, so let us have one evening that we can remember with some semblance of happiness. There is too much between us, too many memories for it to end without that at least.'

They both knew he was talking about Paolo, and although Grace realised that he was using a subtle form of blackmail, that the ruthless side to him that was always there just under his skin was making itself known, she found herself nodding anyway. Because she wanted this evening as much as he did. The only difference being that she loved him, she thought painfully, and he was governed purely by the overwhelming physical attraction that had always been so powerful and fierce between them.

'I don't think it's a good idea, but if you insist. . .' She looked up at him warily, her eyes shadowed with her thoughts.

'I do insist, *mia piccola*.' He smiled, but she didn't trust the apparent good humour. She had seen him smile that way with other folk in the past, just moments before he went in for the kill. He was an intimidating man, she thought tremblingly. And just how intimidating she hadn't realised until she had walked out of his life.

Ridiculous though it would sound to anyone else if she voiced it, she knew his dark aura had reached out to her across the ocean through all the months they had been apart. There had been times when she had almost felt him watching her, breathing over her. . . It *was* ridiculous! She chastised herself firmly for the absurdity of the thought, pushing her fears under lock and key as she tore her eyes away from the magnetic power of his.

He was a man—just a man. She had left once and she could do it again. 'One evening, then,' she said slowly, shrugging herself loose from his hold as she spoke. 'And tomorrow I must arrange my plane ticket home. Lorenzo is much better now, and my job won't be held open forever.'

A ticket back to loneliness, grey days and even greyer nights, an eternity of futile memories and gnawing pain at the thought of what might have been. . .

CHAPTER EIGHT

RINALDI'S was the sort of nightclub that ran under the premise that if any of their clientele had to ask the price of a meal or a drink they couldn't afford to be there, and the establishment was a favourite with the international jet set in the summer. It was a place to see and be seen, to show off the latest Diors and diamonds and one's current partner, to be extravagant, lavish and wasteful. It also boasted the best chef on the whole southern stretch of Italy, a fact which carried more weight with the average Italian than all the other attributes, and Donato was no exception.

'You look very lovely, *mia piccola*.' As Grace stepped through the door into the main house Donato was waiting for her, dark and magnificent in full evening dress, his black hair slicked back and his tanned skin throwing the white of his shirt into brilliant contrast. He looked dangerous, threatening and frighteningly male, and for a moment Grace felt as though she were meeting him for the first time in her life, and her stomach catapulted with the sheer magnetic pull of his masculinity.

'Thank you.' She managed to dredge a weak smile from somewhere, glad that she had dressed for the occasion and that the dress she had chosen, a beautifully cut short cocktail dress in cream brocade, was one Donato had not seen before. She had bought it just days before she'd left Italy the year before, and had left it, along with all her other clothes, when she had fled the country. It suited her, the wafer-thin straps and low neckline emphasising her long neck and slender shoulders and the tininess of her waist. 'You look pretty good yourself,' she said nervously.

'How many times have we dined and danced the night away?' he asked softly. 'Content merely to be with each other? Hundreds I think—thousands, maybe.' He smiled quizzically, his eyes warm.

'A slight exaggeration.' She forced the cool mockery past the thumping of her heart and she knew that he knew. 'And when were we ever alone at Rinaldi's? Everyone wants to be seen to know you,' she added a trifle caustically. 'Especially there.'

'Now it is you who is exaggerating,' he said with a wry grimace, his eyes brilliant on her face. 'I am a very ordinary man, am I not? There is nothing unusual about Donato Vittoria.'

'You don't believe that,' she said disbelievingly, her lips twitching with amusement in spite of the way her heart was aching with love for him. Modesty was not a natural Vittoria trait.

'No, I do not,' he agreed wickedly. 'But I thought it sounded suitably humble.'

She did laugh then, although her amusement was mixed with such pain that it was bitter sweet. He was impossible, he always had been and he always would be, but if it hadn't been for Maria, and his complete lack of remorse about the whole affair, she would be throwing herself into his arms at this very moment.

The air was warm and filled with the scent of lemon groves from the hillsides above as Donato helped her out of the car outside Rinaldi's after telling Antonio he would not be needed for the rest of the night. He took her arm as they walked in, his touch electric.

The nightclub was just as expensive and luxurious as she remembered, with waiters gliding round tables as though on oiled wheels and the flash of diamonds and other precious gems competing with the glittering chandeliers overhead, and the subdued stir that greeted Donato's entrance was familiar too.

He was undeniably the most arresting man in the place, Grace admitted to herself, and women did throw themselves at him *constantly*—something she had never quite got used to in all the time she had known him. But the real crux of the matter was that she had never understood why he had chosen her. There were so many women, beautiful, intelligent wealthy women, who would have taken him on any terms he cared to dictate, so why had he picked out a little nobody from England and married her? It didn't make sense, except that he was a law unto himself. Perhaps that was the answer?

'It is so nice to see you again, Signor Vittoria.' The head waiter was all white teeth and charm as he showed them to their table. 'I will have champagne brought to you immediately.'

A snap of his fingers and the champagne appeared like magic, complete with ice bucket, two crystal glasses and an ingratiating smile, and after the sparkling liquid was poured and they were left alone with their menus Donato leant across the table, taking her small hand in his. 'You hate it, do you not?' he asked softly.

'What?' She stared at him wide-eyed, wondering if he had read her mind again. He had.

'The obsequiousness, the courting of favour.'

'I. . .' She hesitated, a polite, non-committal lie hovering on her lips, and then shrugged slowly. 'Yes, I do,' she said quietly, 'I always have. Don't you?'

'I never really noticed it until I met you.' He settled back in his seat, his eyes intent on her face. 'I grew up with this lifestyle, Grace, it is not foreign to me, and there was a great deal I took for granted. When I met you. . .' He paused, leaning forward again and raising her fingers to his lips in a brief caress. 'You opened my eyes to much I was blind to.'

'*I* did?' She was utterly astonished and he smiled drily.

'You think all the new experiences were solely yours?' he asked gently. 'Grace, you will never know what it meant to me to meet you, so fresh and unspoilt and blatantly honest. I was terrified that you would not marry me, that I might frighten you off in some way. I walked on the——how do you say it?——the eggshells for so long I was in danger of ordering ballet shoes.

'But still I rushed you. . .' He moved restlessly, taking a gulp of champagne that didn't pay sufficient homage to the excellent vintage. 'I knew it but I still did it, because I was afraid of losing you.'

'Losing me?' She couldn't comprehend what he was saying. 'But I loved you, Donato, you know that. I told you often enough.'

'Grace, you were eighteen when we met, but you could have been a child of twelve, thirteen, so innocent were you about the ways of men. I was twenty-five, and I was not innocent.' He looked at her, allowing her to see into his eyes which were dark and cynical.

'I had had women since the age of puberty. I was wealthy, powerful, and reasonable to look at, and such things are an aphrodisiac in the world in which I move. I had friends who were in a similar position to myself and we played the field—'

'I know, you've told me all this before.' It hurt to hear about the other women, even now.

'But you have never understood what it meant to me when I met you, *mia piccola*. Your beauty, your fragility, with an inner core that was so strong—' He broke off, shaking his head slowly. 'I did not believe someone like you existed in the real world, Grace, and I wanted you so much,' he said huskily.

That word again—*want*. She stared at him, her eyes shadowing with pain. She had thought wanting equated with loving, but if he had loved her wouldn't he have waited just a short time for her, until she had climbed out of the pit of black despair and emptiness Paolo's death had thrown her into? She would have managed it, she knew that now, she had nearly been there on the night of her birthday party, when suddenly everything had changed.

One night. *One night*. But perhaps it would have happened anyway, both of them being the people they were? They were so different... 'We're so different.' She echoed her thoughts faintly, almost unaware she was voicing them out loud. 'And there is no going back.'

'We are two parts of one whole.' His voice was low

and urgent. 'And we fit together perfectly. You must believe that.'

Must she? She wanted to, she admitted silently in the deepest recesses of her heart, but her own words reverberated in her head. *Wanting wasn't enough.* She lifted troubled eyes to his and he looked at her intently before executing one of the quicksilver changes she had seen so often in the past, transforming in front of her eyes into a cool, charming dinner companion whose only desire was to keep her amused.

And he did. Whatever he did, Donato did it thoroughly, and in spite of their previous conversation and the gulf between them, which was no more narrow now than when she had returned to Italy, Grace found she was enjoying every mouthful of the delicious dinner as the evening progressed. She was caught up in Donato's spell as completely as she had ever been, despite all the warnings her subconscious was screaming at her.

They had finished dinner and the floor show was just starting, Donato having moved close enough for it to seem natural that his arm was round her shoulders and his thigh warm against hers, when something drew Grace's eyes to the large panelled glass doors at the far end of the room.

Bianca stood there, elegant and breathtakingly lovely in a close-fitting dress of crimson silk, her hair loose and falling down her back in a glossy curtain and her throat and arms alive with jewels. Her eyes had been searching the dimly lit room, but as they fastened on Grace's flame-coloured curls they froze and narrowed, becoming dark pinpoints of light in the pale ivory of her face.

'It's Bianca. . .' She couldn't believe it; she just couldn't believe it.

'What?' Her weak murmur brought Donato's head swinging round to follow her gaze, and she felt him stiffen before he swore softly. But in the next instant Bianca was making her way across the room with a determination that spoke volumes, several male heads following her progress.

'Donato. . .' Bianca was doing her adoring little sister routine to perfection, her eyes bright and her mouth smiling as she reached their table. 'And Grace. This is so nice, that we are all here like this. Romano is just seeing to the taxi. . . Oh, there he is. Catch his attention, Donato, so he knows our table.'

Clever, very clever, Grace thought flatly as Bianca drifted into the seat on the other side of Donato. Don't wait to be asked, assume the invitation is automatic, and there it is—a *fait accompli*. She had a good idea why Bianca had raced into the nightclub ahead of her husband too. Romano was too much of a gentleman to force himself on anyone, let alone his best friend and his estranged wife.

The rest of the evening was an exercise in how to talk poppycock while appearing bright and animated and wearing a Cheshire cat grin. Because in spite of Bianca's subtle intimidation, which was of a nature only another woman could appreciate, Grace was determined to act as though she was enjoying herself.

Most of the time Bianca had a calculating half-smile hovering about her lips, as though she knew something Grace did not, and Grace's unease intensified each time the beautiful slanted eyes slid consideringly over her face.

It was just after Donato had mentioned their leaving, and Grace had excused herself to pop along to the powder room, that the reason for Bianca's mocking, faintly patronising secretive glances became clear. Painfully clear.

Grace was renewing her lipstick at one of the extravagant ornate mirrors in the outer room when the door to the nightclub opened, and she knew immediately whose face would be behind hers when she looked up.

'To be *bella* is not enough, you know this?' Bianca asked contemptuously, tweaking at the lipstick case in Grace's hand with long red-tipped talons and almost flicking it out of her fingers. 'Fire needs to be met with fire.'

'I'm sure you know what you're talking about, Bianca, but frankly I'm not interested.' Grace surveyed her sister-in-law through cold eyes, determined that the other woman wouldn't see how completely she unnerved her. 'Now if you'll excuse me...'

'If I will excuse you?' Bianca made a sound in her throat somewhere between a cackle and a growl. It didn't sound quite human. 'Still the English lady despite everything? Oh, how I despise you! You thought you could fool Madre and all the others, but you do not fool me, you know. It is water that flows through your veins, is it not? Water and ice, not warmth and passion and fire! How did you ever think you could hold a man like Donato—a real man? You should have kept to your own kind.'

'You're sick, Bianca.' Grace's voice held all the revulsion her face was expressing. 'Sick and evil. Now leave me alone.'

'You dare to say that to me because I speak the truth?' Bianca's lips had curled back from her small white teeth in a snarl, her neck stretched forward like a reptile about to strike and her hands claw-like at her side. 'You think you are so superior, so clever—this lady who has everything?'

Everything? What on earth was she talking about? Grace thought helplessly, the savagery of the confrontation numbing her senses. It was Bianca who had everything—a husband, a home, brothers who loved her. She stared at her in fascinated horror.

'But you do not know it all, do you?' A small bubble of saliva escaped the jeering mouth. 'You think he has taken you back into his home because he loves you, *sì*? Because he cares, because he cannot live without you? You are such a fool!'

'I'm going—'

'But it is because Maria has just got engaged to be married and her bed is no longer available to him.'

Grace found she was unable to speak. She wanted to. She wanted to fling a thousand words into the cruel, malicious face in front of her but somehow not one would form in the vacuum that was her mind. She didn't doubt that Bianca was speaking the truth. It would be too easy for her to check on Maria's engagement for Bianca to lie.

'So you see, you are really providing a service. . .for a time.' The black eyes were triumphant as they watched the shock and pain Grace couldn't hide. 'But only for a time,' she added softly.

'Have you finished?' The unnatural calm enabled her to stand straight and proud in front of the Italian woman, her head high and her back stiff as she surveyed Bianca's twisted face.

'*Sì*, I finish.' There was no remorse on Bianca's face, no regret at inflicting such hurt on another human being, merely a diabolical satisfaction at Grace's distress. 'I have said what I came to say.'

'You actually came here tonight just to tell me all that, didn't you?' Grace said slowly. 'What are you, Bianca, what on earth are you? You aren't a woman, that much is for sure, and you are a disgrace to your husband. I pity Romano. I pity him from the bottom of my heart.'

As Bianca went to strike her, Grace stepped forward, her face inches from the enraged woman in front of her. 'Now that I won't allow,' she said softly.

Bianca stared at her with her hand still upraised and her face suffused with ugly colour, and in spite of her brave stance Grace felt something cold and infinitely malignant slither down her spine. There was something wrong—something terribly wrong with Donato's sister. It was staring at her from the narrowed eyes.

Bianca lowered her hand slowly, her gaze never leaving Grace's white face. 'You will regret speaking to me in this way,' she said slowly, with a chilling flatness that was in stark contrast with her fiery countenance. 'I tell you now, you will regret it.'

'Don't threaten me, Bianca,' Grace said steadily, silently praying that her legs would continue to hold her up and that the shaking that was turning her insides to melted jelly would not reveal itself to those piercing eyes. 'I never wanted to be your enemy and you know it. The choice was yours. You disliked me from the day I first came to Casa Pontina, admit it.'

'No, I did not dislike you.' Bianca turned round and walked to the door where she turned, her face vicious. '*I hated you*. I have always hated you. Right from the first moment I saw you I knew you wanted to take my place, to shut me out—'

'That's not true,' Grace protested quickly.

'*Si, si*, it is so. You turned Madre against me. It was all Grace this and Grace that. . .' Bianca paused, and as her face twisted Grace prepared herself for another sword-thrust, but it didn't help when Bianca spat her venom a moment later. 'Even when you let your baby die you could still do no wrong,' she said harshly. 'Even then our lives were still supposed to revolve around you. *Si*, I hate you. I will always hate you.'

'I didn't let him die.' The blow was so severe it caused her to shut her eyes, made her voice a broken whisper. When she opened them again Bianca was walking through the door, and a second later she was alone.

Grace felt herself begin to sway and sank down on one of the spindly-legged quilted chairs in the claustrophobic little room, remaining seated as she leant her head against the cold, hard surface of the mirror in front of her. How long she stayed like that she didn't know, but it was only when the outer door opened again and two women entered that she straightened, pretending to fiddle with her hair as they walked past her into the toilet area beyond after a cursory glance in her direction.

Bianca had touched the wound at its rawest point, and although Grace told herself that the Italian woman was evil, wicked, cruel, that there was no foundation in the accusation, she felt the old panic and horror overwhelm her for sickening minutes until she forced it back by sheer will power, her stomach heaving.

Donato's eyes were looking for her when she walked back into the nightclub, and she saw immediately that Bianca and Romano had gone. 'You are unwell?' He met her halfway across the room, leading her to their table with an arm under her elbow. 'You look very pale,' he said anxiously. 'There is something wrong?'

'No, I'm all right.' She couldn't tell him about the conversation with Bianca in the partying atmosphere all around them, and besides, she thought miserably, what good would it do? She was going to leave Italy within days; she knew that and Donato knew it. He was the one who was going to have to stay here and his sister was part of this life. There had been enough devastation, enough bitterness, and it all seemed to be self-perpetuating. Somewhere, at some point, someone had to say enough was enough. 'Have Bianca and Romano gone?' she asked carefully, her voice neutral.

'Romano has to leave early in the morning for Naples.' He glanced at her, dark eyes alert. 'I thought Bianca said she had told you this?'

'No, I don't think so.' He was going to question her some more, she could see it in the intensity of his gaze, and she spoke quickly before he did. 'Shall we go now? I'm very tired.'

'Of course. The taxi is already waiting,' he said quietly.

She had deliberately made her voice cool and aloof, and once in the taxi answered Donato's attempts at conversation in flat monosyllables, hoping the blatant rebuff would be enough to discourage further probing.

The arrival of Bianca at the nightclub had been enough to shatter the intimate mood that had been between them for the first part of the evening, and now, as she snubbed him again for the third time in as many minutes, she felt his withdrawal as he settled back in his seat in a grim, cold silence that lasted until they reached Casa Pontina.

'Goodnight, thank you for a lovely evening.' On entering the house she turned to make straight for her own quarters, hoping to escape the keen, searching gaze that always seemed to see straight into her mind, but it wasn't to be.

'No way, Grace.' His voice was deep and cold and angry, but also menacingly quiet, which was more

unnerving than any show of rage. 'There is no way I am
going to be frozen out again tonight without an adequate
explanation.'

'What?' As she swung round to face him he moved
swiftly, taking her arm in a grip that was punishing as
he forced her along the hall. 'Let go of me!' she said
helplessly. 'Donato. . .'

'You are going to talk to me tonight—*really* talk to
me,' he said grimly, 'and in the privacy of our own home.
I have had enough, do you understand me? I have finally
had enough. Enough of the gently, gently approach,
enough of the psychology, dammit. I am hurting too, and
I will not let you walk through that door and shut me
out of my home and your heart one more night.'

'You're hurting me!' She tried to pull his fingers from
her arm but in the next moment he had opened the door
to Bambina Pontina and pushed her through, following
straight behind her before locking the door after him and
putting the key in his pocket, his eyes black slits of rage
as he glared at her.

'I would like to hurt you, Grace.' He pulled off his
jacket as he spoke, slinging it across the hall before
loosening his bow tie so it hung in two black strips round
his neck. 'Tonight I would really like to hurt you so that
you know I exist, that I am here, alive, flesh and blood.
Can you understand that?'

'Don't you dare lay a finger on me,' she said tightly.

'You think you can pretend that our marriage never
happened, is that it?' he asked savagely. 'You imagine
that I will allow you to leave, allow another man to touch
you, love you—'

'You don't own me.' She glared at him, her own temper hot and boiling now. So, it was all right for him to
take a mistress when he felt like it and then summon her
back here like some feudal lord, was it? At a time when
it suited him for her to act as nursemaid to his brother,
and conveniently, oh, so *very* conveniently, when his
mistress had finally decided to end their affair? 'Just get
that into your head.'

'I do.' His eyes were fiery but his voice was cold. 'Make no mistake about that, my pale little English rose. I own you. I have owned you since the day we first met, because from that time I would not have allowed another man to have you. I have felt your body quiver beneath mine, heard my name on your lips at the point of ecstasy, seen our son in the moment he was born. Do you think I will ever let you go?'

'You can't keep me here against my will,' she said hotly, her eyes wild. 'Not even you would dare do that.'

'But it will not be against your will.' He moved closer, and in spite of herself she felt her senses leap at the look on his face. 'We both know that when I touch you it will not be against your will, don't we, *mia piccola*?' he asked softly.

'I'm leaving as soon as I've booked a flight.' She saw the ebony eyes widen for a second at the panic and alarm in her voice, and then he shook his head slowly, his gaze stroking over her burning face.

'Then you leave me no alternative,' he said huskily. 'Desperate times need desperate measures, *si*? And this is a desperate time, Grace. A time when I have to convince you that you belong to me as I do to you, that we are meant to be together. Paolo was a blessing given to us for a short time only, but I will not allow our son's memory to be the wedge that keeps us apart.'

'But it isn't Paolo—'

He cut off her voice by taking her mouth in a kiss that betrayed the raging hunger within, devouring her as he held her locked against him so tightly she couldn't move. She felt an exhilarating heat mixed with a fierce, shameful excitement as the blood turned to fire in her veins and she fought it with all her might. She was determined not to weaken before the sensual power of the man, but time began to lose its meaning as desire rose.

'Grace, Grace. . .' He was murmuring against her mouth now, his breathing ragged. 'I do not want to take you against your will, you know this. I love you, *mia piccola*, I will always love you. Do not keep us apart.

Paolo's death was a tragedy but we were not to blame—
you were not to blame—you must believe this. No one
could have loved him more than you did, and small
though he was he knew that. He had more love in his
short life than some people have in a lifetime.'

It was what she needed to hear, with Bianca's cruel
poison still caustic in her mind, and although she knew
it was madness his words swept away the last of her
resistance. She turned her head, searching for his lips,
sliding her arms up to his neck and feeling him shudder
against her as she pressed her softness against the hard,
strong body that was already on fire for her.

He had said he loved her and maybe he did, in his
way. She had fought and fought and now there was no
fight left inside her. She wanted the reassurance of his
love to banish the nightmare she had lived in for so long,
she told herself feverishly. She needed him. She needed
his strength and security and physical sovereignty,
needed to feel safe, protected. . .

'Oh, my darling, my darling.' He lifted her up into his
arms as though she were thistledown, his lips taking hers
again as he walked up the stairs to the room they had
shared so many, many tears ago.

He was gentle as he placed her on the bed, in spite
of the consuming passion that was revealed in all its
magnificence as he finished undressing and joined her
on the covers, helping her out of her own clothes with
a tenderness that bordered on reverence.

She clung to him as she felt the surging strength of
his big naked body against hers, her breath coming in
short panting gasps as his hands moved over her swollen
breasts, the curve of her thighs, the silky skin of her arms
and legs, in an agony of exploration that spoke of denial.

'I have never stopped wanting you for one moment,'
he whispered thickly, 'not one. I have seen you in my
dreams, night after night, spread out before me like this.
I have imagined you sobbing out with desire beneath my
caresses.'

She answered by touching him in such a way that

shivers of pleasure shook his body, and then as he lowered his head to pay homage to the hardened peaks of
her breasts she moaned in pleasure, unable to control the
trembling that had taken her over.

And then there were no more words beyond incoherent
murmurings as molten feeling surged between them, his
hands and mouth ravaging the secret places only he had
possessed, their bodies shuddering together as he urged
them on and on to the very brink of fulfilment, only to
slow down again until she was sobbing his name against
his lips. 'Please, Donato, please. . .'

'Soon, soon, my love.' His voice was a shaken whisper
against the silk of her skin. 'We have waited so long for
this night, suffered so much, it has to be right.'

When he lifted her to him it was because their agony
of need had reached a pitch of unbearable pleasure, the
touching and tasting and caressing bringing her to a moist
quivering that heralded her readiness. But in spite of the
years of marriage, the bearing of a child, she was very
tight as his swollen power surged between her thighs and
he stilled instantly, his arms taking the weight of his
body as he raised himself slightly to look into her face.
'Do you want me to stop?' he asked huskily, his eyes
narrowed with the restraint that was tensing his muscles
like steel.

'No. . .' She couldn't say any more, the delicious
rhythmic contractions that his invasion had started gath-
ering momentum in such a way that her body talked for
itself. And as he felt her pleasure, her complete sub-
mission to his manhood, he began to move harder and
faster, creating an exquisite surging tide of sensation in
which there was no room for anything but the moment.

She called his name at the peak of fulfilment although
she wasn't aware of it, the world of colour and light and
blinding ecstasy beyond anything she had known before,
beyond anything she had imagined.

As the pounding of his heart began to quieten and their
breathing steadied he moved gently from her, turning
onto his side and pulling her within the curve of his body

with her back resting against the hard wall of his chest. 'Sleep, my love, he murmured softly as her trembling ceased and she relaxed against him. 'Just sleep now. You are home again and everything is going to be all right. I promise you this.'

It wasn't, she knew it wasn't, but the physical and mental exhaustion that had her in its grip was too consuming to fight, and anyway, it was wonderfully comforting to be enfolded in the familiar smell and feel of him, to let her mind drift away into the warm blanket of sleep knowing she was held close to his heart.

Grace awoke when it was still dark, the confusing, disturbing dream she had been entangled in telling her tired mind that something was dreadfully wrong. And then, as she moved slightly and felt the warm body at the side of her, she knew.

Donato. She had done the one thing she had promised herself she would never do. She had let him into her bed and her heart again. Useless to say now that it had been in the heat of the moment, that Bianca's cruel spite had lowered her defences, had exposed the vulnerability that was ever present around this man she loved so much, that his gentle understanding of her need to be comforted about the loss of their child and his profession of love had tipped the precarious balance. She had made love with him, allowed him to think that she was his again, and she knew now, even more than before, that it could never be.

His power over her was absolute and his magnetic pull as strong as ever. This in spite of the fact that nothing had been sorted between them. Maria's name was still unmentioned and his infidelity had not been spoken of. She was committing emotional suicide, and she couldn't go through the last twelve months again. If she went back to him now it would be without any reassurance for the future, with no guarantee that the same thing wouldn't happen again.

He hadn't reassured her, asked her forgiveness,

explained anything. He had simply beckoned and she had fallen into his arms. She shut her eyes tightly and stifled the moan in her throat. How could she have been so stupid? How could she?

'Grace?' His voice was sleepy against the back of her neck, but he must have sensed the tensing of her body as her thoughts burnt into her soul. 'You are awake?' he asked tenderly.

'Yes.' Useless to prevaricate. Perhaps what she had to say would be best said under the cover of darkness.

'Darling—'

'No!' As he made to turn her to face him she rolled swiftly off the bed, reaching for her robe which was draped over a chair close by. 'I. . .I have to explain,' she said nervously.

'Explain?' He laughed softly. 'Come back to bed, *mia piccola*, and I will listen to what you have to say.'

His voice was indulgent, lazy, and panicked her still more. She couldn't have him; she mustn't let herself be drawn into anything more. He had to *see*. 'No, you don't understand,' she said stumblingly. 'Last night was a mistake. It should never have happened. We. . . It doesn't change anything—it can't.'

'Grace?' The light, easy warmth was fading, and the next moment the bedside lamp was clicked on to flood the room with a rosy glow. Donato had sat up, careless of his nakedness, the sheet falling in folds about his thighs and his magnificent broad chest causing her muscles to tighten. 'What the hell is going on?' he asked quietly.

'I. . .I shouldn't have slept with you last night,' she said feverishly, struggling into the robe and pulling the belt tight as she spoke.

'The hell you shouldn't.' He still didn't realise exactly what she was saying, the mildness of his tone telling her he was humouring what he saw as her morning-after nerves. 'We are married, remember?' he said teasingly. 'You are allowed to have my body.'

'You know what I mean.' She cast agonised eyes in

his direction before sinking onto the chair, her legs trembling so much they wouldn't support her. There followed a moment of loud silence.

'No, I do not know what you mean,' he said quietly, the expression on her face having convinced him this was more than just a brief panic. 'Perhaps you would like to tell me? Call me old-fashioned, but I always thought making love was something married couples did fairly often, and considering the last time we indulged was more than twelve months ago I did not think I was being overly. . .demanding?'

'We didn't make love.' She couldn't let him term it as such when it meant something so different to him. 'We. . .'

'Well?' he asked flatly when she didn't continue, her face scarlet. 'What exactly *did* we do, then? Spell it out for me, Grace, because I am either damned stupid or I am missing something vital here. As far as I was concerned last night I was making love to my wife. What were you doing?'

'Don't put it like that,' she said hotly, resentment flaring through her at the contempt in his voice. How dared he? How *dared* he act as if she was the immoral one? 'You can't blame me for thinking it didn't mean much to you—not after Maria.'

'Maria?' He was out of the bed in one movement, striding across to her and hauling her up out of the chair to stand in front of him, dark colour flaring across the high cheekbones and his eyes glittering slits of black light. 'What has Maria to do with this?'

'What has. . .?' She was so angry, so enraged at his feeble attempt to evade the real issue between them that she could barely form the words. '*Maria Fasola*,' she ground out through clenched teeth. 'Remember her? Bianca's little friend? The woman who has so recently decided to go for respectability rather than the dubious pleasure of your bed? I think she has everything to do with this, don't you?'

'I haven't the faintest idea what you are talking about.'

And as he said it there was something—an inflexion
in his voice, the expression on his face—that told her
something was dreadfully, terrifyingly wrong. 'But I
think it is time for this explaining of which you spoke,'
he continued, with a menacing coldness that chilled her
blood. 'Although I think it is going to tell me that I have
been the worst sort of fool.'

'I. . . You. . . The letter. . .' She was frightened of him,
she realised with a little shock of horror. For the first
time in her life she was frightened of him, of the bitter
fury and hurt in his eyes, of the lethal set to his mouth—
that mouth that had taken her to heaven and back just a
few hours before.

'What letter?' He let go of her arms as he spoke, but
with a savagery that jerked her from him before he bent
down and picked up his trousers, discarded in such passion the night before. 'What letter, Grace?' he repeated
slowly when she didn't speak, grinding the words out
with a control that was paper-thin.

'The letter I left the day I went back to England,' she
said desperately. 'Where I explained everything.'

'There was no letter.' He faced her, clothed in the
black trousers, his feet and torso bare and his hair ruffled,
the black stubble on his chin accentuating his masculinity. He looked wonderful—wonderful and majestic
and terrifying. And she had lost him for the last and final
time, she realised dully.

'But I left a letter,' she stumbled on, knowing she was
making things a hundred times worse but unable to stop.
'Saying that I had found out about your affair with Maria,
that I was leaving you. Why. . .why did you think I'd
left if you didn't find the letter?'

'I thought you left Italy because it had become too
painful for you to stay,' he said grimly. 'Because the
loss of our child was weighing so heavily you needed to
put distance between yourself and everything that was
associated with him for a time.'

'Donato—'

'But you thought I had taken a mistress?' He spoke

as if the idea was so incredible, so bizarre as to be impossible. 'Our child had been taken from us, you were almost suicidal, and you thought I had taken a *mistress*?' he ground out slowly.

For the first time the possibility that Donato hadn't betrayed her, that somehow, somewhere there had been a cataclysmic mistake dawned, but there was no relief, no wild deliverance at the thought. Because it was too late. The bitter contempt and fury in his eyes told her that. He would never forgive her for believing it.

'Since the first day I met you I have never looked at another woman,' he said tightly. 'You filled my days and my nights; there was no room for anyone else. I thanked God every day that you had come into my life, do you know that, Grace?' he asked with bitter self-contempt. 'And all the time you were watching me, expecting me to fail you.'

'No.' She stared at him aghast. 'It wasn't like that.'

'No?' He shook his head slowly. 'I do not believe you. Who told you I was having an affair? I presume someone did?'

'Yes.' Bianca's name trembled on her lips but she just didn't know how to say it, to tell him that his own flesh and blood had conspired to destroy their marriage. Would he believe her anyway? she asked herself frantically. Knowing what she knew now, it was more than possible that Bianca would deny everything. Why, oh, why hadn't she unburdened herself to Liliana that day, told her the reason she was leaving? Perhaps then they might have had a chance?

'But you are not going to tell me who,' he stated grimly after a few moments. 'You took the word of this person without any proof, without even speaking to me, and you simply walked out of my life, and now you ask me to believe you were not expecting me to betray you at some point? There was no letter, was there, Grace? You just wanted me out of your life.'

'No, Donato, no.' She had thought she had seen him in all his moods during the years they had been together, but this bitter self-disgust, the smouldering, dangerous rage, the sheer fury was something new. 'Please, it wasn't like that. There *was* a letter—'

'And I thought I had to let you go for a time,' he continued cuttingly. 'That I had to make that great self-sacrifice so you could gain some peace and inner strength and see how things really were.

'I could see living with me was making you worse but I thought it was because of Paolo, because I had rushed you into marriage before you had had time to mature, because Paolo had arrived too quickly, because you were blaming yourself for his death—oh, a thousand and one things. And I believed they were all my fault.

'My mother thought the same, did you know that?' he asked bitterly. 'On the night of your birthday party, when you left so early, we had a long talk and we agreed it was best I back off for a while, that I loved you too much to be able to help you, that I had to give you space. Liliana was going to be there for you.'

'But. . .but you didn't say,' she murmured weakly. 'I thought you had had enough of the way I had been—'

'*Damn you, Grace!*' The words slammed into her with the force of bullets. 'You thought I was that shallow? I loved you, woman, I would have given my life to stop you hurting the way you were. I could not bear the fact that you had suffered such unhappiness before you met me, that it had screwed up your view of yourself so badly. Hell!' He drove his fist into the palm of his hand. 'What sort of a man do you think I am? Why did you marry me in the first place if your opinion of me is so damn low?' he asked, with an anguish that cut her in two.

'It isn't—it wasn't—'

'The hell it isn't,' he ground out savagely. 'For the last twelve months—longer—you have been thinking I had a mistress. That—*that*—is the truth. And all the time I was thinking I had to let you go for a while because I cared so much, this idea was fermenting in your brain. You do not love me, Grace. I doubt if you ever loved me.' He was looking at her as though he had never seen her before.

She wanted to deny it, to tell him that he was everything to her, that the last twelve months away from him had all but killed her, but the knowledge of how badly she had let him down had hit her like a violent blow in the solar plexus, and his contempt was numbing. How could she have been so blind? How *could* she?

And as she stood silently searching for words, trying to force something past the sick self-disgust and guilt that were constricting her throat and drying her thought processes, he walked straight past her and out of the door, shutting it quietly—painfully quietly—behind him.

CHAPTER NINE

FOR the remainder of the night Grace sat on the balcony, staring at the dark canopy above punctured by thousands upon thousands of twinkling lights as she searched for some reason, some logic to explain Bianca's corrosive interference in their lives.

Had Donato's sister really believed he was having an affair with Maria? she asked herself wearily. She knew Maria had always wanted him. Perhaps the beautiful Italian girl had lived in a fantasy world where what she desired had become real, to the point where she had confided the supposed affair to the ear of her best friend, Donato's sister?

Or had Bianca herself been so jealous of her brother's wife's place in the Vittoria family that she had engineered the whole series of events, striking at a time when she must have been well aware that the loss of Paolo had rendered Grace desperately vulnerable and insecure?

She didn't want to believe that, Grace thought helplessly. She didn't want to believe she had inspired such dislike, such hate, but she just wasn't sure.

A soft pastel dawn began to streak the night sky with pink and mauve as memories, buried for the sake of family harmony, now surfaced. Painful, hurtful memories—memories that burnt like acid.

Bianca's face, scarlet with outrage, when Donato had announced their engagement, followed by her initial refusal to be matron of honour, despite the fact Donato had asked Romano to be his best man. Romano had taken his wife for a walk in the grounds, she remembered now, and by the time they had returned Bianca had been grudgingly acquiescent to the wedding plans—although Grace had known even then that it was only because Romano had insisted on her behaving well.

From that point Bianca's antagonism had gone underground, only surfacing when the two of them were alone, but it had been none the less vitriolic for that.

But would Bianca actually have fabricated such a terrible lie, woven all the threads in place with such cunning and dexterity? Grace asked herself as her stomach churned over and over. It was one thing to believe the hopeful fantasies of a friend and repeat them as fact to someone you disliked, quite another to set out to destroy a marriage—your own brother's marriage at that. What would Bianca gain by such cruelty? It wasn't as though she lived at Casa Pontina any more. She had her own home with Romano, a separate identity, a life of her own.

'It can't be true.' Grace spoke out loud into the softness of the early morning, a thousand summer scents perfuming the fresh, warm air that promised another baking hot day. It couldn't. . .could it? But something, or, more to the point, someone, had got them to where they were now, and suddenly Bianca seemed to be holding the key.

She went down to breakfast without any clear decision or plan in her mind, and it was only when she found Lorenzo alone, spooning a hefty helping of golden scrambled egg onto his plate, that things began to crystallise.

'Donato's not down yet, then?' she asked the small boy with elaborate casualness, her heart pounding violently against her ribcage. She would grovel, plead, beg—anything, she told herself painfully. Anything at all if it could send them back just twenty-four hours in time.

But it couldn't. What had been said was said, and nothing could take it back. He must hate her now, really hate her.

'I think he must have already left, Grace,' Lorenzo said with cheerful innocence, not knowing he was crushing the last faint hope she'd had that Donato still cared enough to give her a second chance. 'I knocked on his door this morning but there was no answer, and when I looked inside his room it was empty. He sometimes has to leave very early, you know,' he added seriously, with all the dignity of a true Vittoria. 'He is a very important man.'

'I know.' Just how important she had never fully realised until this very moment, when she accepted that he had walked out of her life for good. But she loved him, she would die loving him, and one thing she *was* going to do was find out exactly what had gone on between Bianca and Maria.

It wouldn't do any good now, but she had to know the truth before she left Italy. She had lost Donato, the blow she had given to his love and his pride—oh, yes, that devastatingly iron-hard Vittoria pride—had been too much. He would never forgive her, and perhaps she didn't deserve his forgiveness, she told herself wretchedly.

Against all the odds she had been given paradise and she had thrown it away. She should have known. *She should have known*, she repeated desperately to herself, that the man she loved, the man who had nurtured her, supported her, cared for her and loved her far beyond anything she had dreamed of, was not capable of the treachery and shallowness she had suspected.

His motives had been noble in letting her go without more bitterness, more heart-searing quarrels, and all the time she had been in England he had been caring for her still, making sure she was safe, and she had even thrown that in his face.

She recalled her fury when she had discovered he had had her watched and had to stifle an agonised groan at the memory, conscious of Lorenzo's presence across the table as he scoffed ham and scrambled eggs.

'You *paid* someone to spy on me.' That was what she had said. 'What gives you the right to think you can act like that? It's immoral.' And his reaction to the accusation had been an icy withdrawal, a refusal to try and explain himself.

And now, after this latest revelation, the withdrawal would be complete. Being a Vittoria he couldn't let it be anything else, she thought painfully.

Signor de' Medici, Lorenzo's handsome young tutor,

arrived as Lorenzo finished his last mouthful of food, and then after a few minutes of polite conversation that Grace conducted automatically, her mind in a different realm altogether, she was alone again. She sat gazing at the array of dishes lining the sideboard for a minute or two more, although she knew she couldn't eat a bite. She didn't feel as if she'd ever eat again.

'Good morning.'

She jumped so violently as the deep, dark voice sounded behind her that her knees made painful contact with the top of the breakfast table, and then Donato strolled into view, walking across to the sideboard and beginning to fill his plate without glancing in her direction.

He was wearing his regulation breakfast gear, short grey towelling robe and little else, and his hair was still damp from the shower. Her heart gave the sort of leap that won gold medals before pounding in her chest cavity like a sledge-hammer, and she opened her mouth twice before she could force anything out. 'I thought. . .I thought you'd already left,' she said breathlessly.

'Did you?' He still didn't turn round. 'I am sorry to disappoint you but it was necessary to do some work here first. I intended to do it last night but I got. . . distracted.' He did turn then, his dark eyes moving over her with a cool remoteness that registered like a slap in the face. 'You know how it is.'

'Oh, I see. You were in your study, then? That explains it,' she said confusedly, her mind still reverberating with the shock and pain of that supremely uninterested glance. In all the years she had known him he had looked at her in many ways, with love, with anger, amusement, tenderness and a hundred other emotions besides, but never, *never* as though he didn't care. Until now.

His eyes narrowed slightly, but otherwise the blankness remained. 'Explains what?' he asked smoothly.

'Lorenzo came to your room but you weren't there, so he assumed you'd already left. . .' Her faltering voice died away under the dark, expressionless stare. It was like talking to someone who wasn't really there, a robot.

'Lorenzo. . .yes, I see.' He pulled out a chair, sitting down opposite her and beginning to eat a warm croissant with every appearance of enjoyment. 'He is with Signor de' Medici?' he asked distantly.

'Yes.' Oh, this was awful, she told herself desperately. She had to say something, *do* something to break through that terrible Vittoria ice. They had to talk at least. 'I. . .I don't know how much longer you think I should stay here with Lorenzo,' she said nervously, immediately berating herself with deep scorn for her cowardice.

She wanted to beg him to forgive her, promise him the sun, moon and stars, but this new Donato was more intimidating and frightening than she had ever imagined; she could see now how he had taken over his father's empire with such ease. From the moment he had walked into the room she had felt herself begin to shrink back into the scared little girl of her childhood, and although she told herself it was ridiculous, that this was her husband, that she had to fight now for their marriage or spend the rest of her life in misery without him, the formative years of tight bondage closed in on her with steel bands.

'You are asking my opinion?' As the glittering black eyes met hers she saw, just for an instant, something dark and hot and smouldering deep within, before the shutter came slamming back into place. 'Why ask advice from someone you despise so much?' he continued tightly. 'Ask Bianca, or Gina, or Anna—even the man who comes to clean the pool. I am sure you can trust their counsel far better than mine.'

'Don't. . .don't be like this,' she whispered brokenly, her eyes huge in the whiteness of her face. 'Please. . .'

'Like what?' He stood now, the bitter hell he had endured for the last few hours making him want to hurt and wound in retaliation against the pain. 'How am I supposed to be, Grace? You tell me, spell it out, because I would really like to know. I thought we were one in soul and body, that nothing and no one could ever drive us apart, that you were the other part of me without which I could not be whole, but it was all lies, was it not? We were strangers—we *are* strangers.'

'Donato—'

'I gave you everything. Oh, not this—' he flung a contemptuous hand at the luxury surrounding them '—I do not mean this, I mean myself—my mind, my soul, the inner core that I had never revealed to another living person. I gave it to you without hesitation and I thought you had given me the same, but all the time you were outside looking on.'

'No, it wasn't like that,' she said desperately. 'Listen to me, Donato—'

'Grace, you have told me what it was like,' he said, with a deep weariness that was worse than his rage. 'You believed vicious gossip, *rumours*, so completely that you did not even come to me to ask if there was any truth in what you had heard. Shortly after Paolo was taken from us Maria came to the Naples office as secretary to one of my directors, I have seen her once or twice at her desk or in the lift; that is all.'

'I. . .I see.'

'No, you do not see, Grace, you do not see at all. I did not know Erminio had even hired her until I saw her in his office, but even if I had known I would not have considered it a problem. She is nothing to me—*nothing*.'

'Donato—'

'If you suspected something untoward you could have asked me about her, made your own enquiries, but I was not worth that sort of effort. You decided I was guilty of this crime and you simply walked away from me. That—that—is the bottom line.'

The flat statement pierced her through, but the truth in it was undeniable. She had no defence against it. 'I'm sorry,' she whispered wretchedly. 'I'm so sorry.'

'And you stayed away.' It took superhuman effort to keep the pain that had ravaged his mind for the last few hours out of his voice. 'And you would have continued to stay away if Madre had not died, would you not? I thought I was giving you time to adjust before you came home, and you were busy making a new life without me.'

His anger rose in such a virulent flood that he knew he had to get out of the room before he said or did something he would regret later. She had rejected him, utterly, completely, without giving him a chance to say anything in his own defence. She had simply left him. And the terrible irony of it all, the most galling thing, was that she was supposed to be the weak one, the sensitive one who needed his strength and protection. But he could never have left her. . . Damn it. *Damn it.*

Grace didn't say a word as he strode out of the room. There was nothing left to say after all. She just sat there with her hands in her lap and her eyes staring blindly ahead, her heart cut to ribbons.

She was still sitting in numb silence a few minutes later, when Gina bustled in to clear the breakfast dishes, and she quickly forced herself to reach for her glass and drink her orange juice in as natural a manner as she could manage as the little Italian maid glanced her way.

'*Scusi, signora.*' Gina made to leave the room again. 'It all quiet and I think everyone finished. *Scusi.*'

'It's all right, Gina.' It was amazing how she could smile and talk when the screaming inside her was so loud. 'I was just going,' she said calmly, praying the control would hold.

'I take Benito his papaw, *si*? He bad bird, but I give him the papaw every morning.' The maid lifted the lid of the dish and spooned out several slices. 'He tells me if I am late,' she added ruefully.

'I'll take it if you like, Gina.' Grace took the dish from the girl as she spoke. 'I know you're a bit frightened of him but he doesn't bother me, really. I'd like to feed him this morning,' she said quietly.

'You sure, *signora*?' Gina's relief was transparent. Both the maids were very respectful of the bad-tempered, irascible old parrot, and being the wily bird he was Benito capitalised fully on their fear, ruling them with a rod of iron.

'Of course. I'll take it now.' She rose as she spoke, and hurried along to the sitting room, knowing Lorenzo would be ensconced with Signor de' Medici in the room next door—Benito having proved too much of a distraction when Lorenzo had attempted to have his lessons in his own room.

The parrot was sitting watching the door as she entered, bright round eyes knowing exactly what they were looking for, and immediately he spied the dish of papaw he began to jig excitedly along his perch, his harsh voice demanding, '*Frutta, frutta, mmm.*' He made a sound very like a small boy smacking his lips in pleasure, and in spite of her misery Grace smiled at the irrepressible old bird. He really was one on his own!

'Yes, here's your *frutta*, you wicked old tyrant,' she said fondly, handing him a piece which he took with remarkable gentleness before devouring it with great relish.

She had just given him his second piece when the telephone rang shrilly at her side, the extension being on the small table she had placed Benito's papaw on. She picked it up automatically, her mind still dissecting every word and intonation Donato had uttered.

'Signora Vittoria.' The voice was autocratic and cold as it asked for her, and unmistakably Bianca's. She always used that tone with the maids.

'Bianca? This is Grace speaking.' Grace sat down rather suddenly on the chair by the telephone, much to the dismay of Benito, who eyed the remaining papaw longingly, but just hearing that sharp, imperious voice had turned her stomach. 'I was actually going to ring you later,' she said carefully. 'We need to talk.'

'*Sì?*' The word was tight and guarded. 'You are alone, Grace?' Bianca asked coldly. 'There is no one with you?'

'No, there's no one here.' Grace held the smooth plastic more tightly. This clearly wasn't a conciliatory call, not that she had expected one after the confrontation last night, but it would have been easier if Bianca had met her halfway in view of what she had to ask. But the frosted tones told their own story. 'Bianca, I want to know—'

'I phone to ask when you leave Italy,' Bianca interrupted with a burning hostility that shot down the line. 'You say you have the job, the life in England? So, when do you go back, eh?'

'What?' Grace stared down at the receiver as she moved it away from her face, unable to believe she had heard right.

'I think it is time you go.' The disembodied voice seemed to be quite unaware of the outrageous audacity of the words, and there suddenly surged in Grace a fury, an overwhelming rage that quelled the trembling in her stomach and put steel in her voice.

'Oh, do you, indeed?' She paused for a moment, and from the blank silence on the other end of the telephone it was clear Bianca had caught her mood. 'You seem to be forgetting one tiny thing, Bianca. This is my home and Donato is my husband,' she said sharply.

'Huh!' The exclamation was contemptuous. 'You say this after you leave him—after you run away? You have a home in England now, you tell me this, and Donato does not love you any more. There is nothing for you in Italy.'

'Perhaps I disagree with that.'

There was an inflexion in Grace's voice that caused a sharp intake of breath on the other end of the line, and then Bianca said, her voice deadly soft, 'You are telling me you are together again, is that it? As man and wife?'

'I wasn't aware I was "telling" you anything, Bianca. I don't have to; it's none of your business,' Grace said steadily.

'*Si—si*, it is my business! Donato, he is my brother—'

'And he is *my* husband,' Grace shot back hotly, 'and whether you like it or not this is my home. And I tell you now you're not welcome in it any more, Bianca. I don't know what Maria has said to you, but I do know you have deliberately tried to part Donato and I.'

'You cannot keep me from Casa Pontina. I have more

right than you to live within its walls,' Bianca snarled furiously. 'You try to turn Donato against me—I know it. Take him away from me like you did Madre and Lorenzo. I am not stupid like the others. I know what you do.'

'You can't really believe that.' The trembling had started again at the sheer malignant rage in Bianca's voice. 'I didn't take Liliana or Lorenzo away from you— how could I, for goodness' sake? They are your family. Donato is your brother—'

'I know what they are!'

'Bianca, it was all lies about Maria, wasn't it? It wasn't her who told you she was having an affair with Donato, you made it all up.' It was a long shot, but such was Bianca's fury Grace felt the Italian woman might admit the truth in her rage.

There was a deep silence, broken only by Benito leaping agitatedly from one foot to another as he caught the atmosphere, his distress compounded by the fact that the papaw was so near and yet so far, and that his old enemy's name had been mentioned far more than he would like.

'You tell Donato I say this?' Bianca asked at last, in a flat monotone that was in stark contrast to the blazing anger of before. 'You talk about me?'

'No, not yet. But it is true, isn't it?' Grace said shakily. 'You kept on at me for months with hints and sly jibes before that day when I asked you straight out about Maria. I know the truth now so you might just as well admit it.'

'No!' It was a sharp snap, and then there was a slight pause before Bianca said, her voice quieter now. 'You do not understand, Grace, it is not as you say. You must listen to me, *si*? We must talk about these things.'

'Go ahead, I'm listening.' Even now Grace harboured a faint hope that Donato's sister would be able to explain away her part in the whole trauma, that she would prove she had been more sinned against than sinful.

'Not on the telephone,' Bianca said softly. 'It is better

that we talk face to face, *si*? Privately, just the two of us? Why do you not come to my house, and I will make the coffee and then we will talk?'

'I. . .I don't know. Can't you come here?' She didn't want to face Bianca on her own territory, she realised with a little stab of disgust at her cowardice, but Donato's sister had thoroughly unnerved her last night, and after the emotional roller coaster of the last few hours she was having a job to think straight. Furthermore, she would need all her wits about her when dealing with the Italian woman. She had been far too trusting in the past, she could see that now, and she could also see where it had got her.

'It is better you come here. We will not be disturbed and at Casa Pontina there is always the activity, *si*? There are things you do not understand, Grace, about Maria. I think she is a little sick, you know? I am her friend and she talks to me, and now I must explain to you.' Bianca's voice was almost gentle, and patiently reasonable, and for the life of her Grace couldn't think of a concrete reason not to go.

'All right.' Bianca was Donato's sister after all, and Grace had to do all she could to try and untangle this mess. 'But I know she didn't sleep with him,' she added firmly. 'Donato's told me that.'

'*Si, si*.' It was said placatingly. 'I understand now.'

'I'll come now, shall I?' Grace asked slowly, wishing she could feel this meeting was a good idea.

'*Si*—and Grace?'

'Yes?' Grace's eyes narrowed. What now?

'It is better that you say nothing to anyone about coming here. Suggest you are going into town, maybe doing a little shopping. That way we will not be interrupted,' Bianca said gently.

Grace found Antonio with Gina and Anna in the kitchen enjoying a cup of coffee, and he immediately went to the board that held the keys to all the cars when he heard her request, handing her the keys to the smart red Fiat coupé Donato had bought her just after Paolo was born.

She kept to the story of going into town, knowing Antonio would be driving Donato to his offices soon and would be sure to mention that she had taken her car, and left the house quickly before Donato came downstairs again.

The morning sun was warm on her arms as she walked across the pleasantly shaded courtyard at the back of the villa to the row of garages where the Vittoria cars were housed, and already the sky was a stunningly vivid blue without a cloud to be seen.

Grace had chosen the coupé herself and now, as she saw it again for the first time in months, the sleek, stylish bonnet and radical lines of the car reproached her for her neglect. It started immediately and she breathed a sigh of relief—the last thing she wanted was to be sitting here when Antonio came for the Mercedes—and drove slowly out of the grounds. She quickly refamiliarised herself with the controls, wondering if she was doing the right thing in visiting the Bellini villa. She didn't trust Bianca, not for a moment.

Nevertheless, she had to talk to Donato's sister, she told herself flatly as she concentrated on the road ahead, and then, when she was in possession of the full facts, she would repeat them to Donato. . .if he would listen to her. She wouldn't blame him if he chose not to; she had been such a blind fool.

The Bellini villa was situated in the Sant' Agnello district of Sorrento, among the fragrant orange groves that made up a large part of Romano's estate, and as Grace drove through narrow, winding streets past sunny pavement cafés, pretty piazzas, fascinating alleyways and numerous flamboyant shops, the butterflies in her stomach were going haywire.

She hated confrontation, having shrunk from its potentially destructive power for the whole of her childhood in the home, but now she saw that this showdown with Bianca had been inevitable from day one. Bianca had been determined to dislike and resent her, and just why she didn't know, but perhaps if she had been more aggressive in the very beginning, had demanded respect and consideration as Donato's wife, things might be different now? But she was as she was, and the sort of belligerence and hard doggedness it would have taken to penetrate Bianca's hostility just weren't in her make-up.

But she had to be strong now. She had to get to the bottom of all the lies and deceit for Donato's sake as much as her own; she owed him that at least.

The sting of tears at the back of her eyes brought her teeth clenching as she forced them back. She couldn't cry now, mustn't. Now was not the time to take on board what the future held, a future without Donato; she had to see Bianca and that needed all her concentration, one second, one minute at a time until the thing was done.

The gates to the Bellini villa were open when she arrived and she drove through them slowly, bringing the car to a standstill in the courtyard at the front of the house.

The villa had been in Romano's family for several generations—the Bellini family tree was as old and noble as the Vittorias'—and the house was very beautiful. The cream-painted walls were mellow and tranquil in the warm morning air and festooned with trailing bougainvillea and dark red ivy, the leaded windows and wrought-iron balconies giving a timelessness to the place that was further enhanced by a cascading stone fountain in the middle of the courtyard and a large white dovecot complete with fat doves.

Grace sat for a moment in the car as the sound of the engine died. The sweet smell of richly perfumed flowers, the tinkling of the running water and the soft, melodious cooing of the resident doves was a stark contrast to the discord she sensed was in front of her.

She had barely put one foot outside the car when the heavy, ornately carved front door swung open to reveal Bianca standing in the aperture, her slim body clothed in a long, clinging dress of virginal white and her black hair looped high on her head, secured with combs in which were threaded tiny white flowers. She looked as exquisite as always, cool and graceful, but not for the first time Grace found herself searching the beautiful features for some softness, humanity even, but there was none.

'*Ciao*, Grace.' Bianca's smile didn't reach the slanted black eyes. 'Come in, please.'

'Thank you.' Ridiculous in the circumstances, Grace thought wryly, to be thanking the possible perpetrator of all her misery.

The interior of the house was as beautiful as the outside, all golden wood floors, elegant furnishings and bowls of sweetly scented flowers, and the long, sprawling sitting room into which Bianca led her had its large French windows open to the perfume and warmth of the gardens beyond.

'So you came.' Bianca's expression was unusual in that it was wary as she turned and faced her, but her words were as aggressive as always as she continued, 'I wondered if you would have the courage.'

'Courage is not a trait exclusive to Italians,' Grace said quietly as she stared straight into the other woman's eyes. This was going to be every bit as bad as she had feared. 'Besides which, I believe Donato—that he has never had an affair with Maria—so whatever you have to say can't be as bad as that.'

'Did you tell anyone you were coming here?' Bianca asked flatly.

'No, we agreed—'

'*Sì*, I know what we agreed, and of course you would keep your word. Pure Grace, lovely Grace, noble Grace—'

'If you just want to turn this into another fight I am leaving now, Bianca,' Grace said, with a firmness that surprised herself.

That it had surprised the Italian woman too was evident when Bianca checked what she had been about to say, swallowing deeply and wetting her lips before she said, 'No, I do not want to fight, Grace. I want to explain.'

'So, explain.'

'Sit down, I will bring in the coffee,' Bianca said stiffly, and as Grace seated herself in a large easy chair close to the open French doors she disappeared for a few moments, returning almost immediately with the coffee-tray. She waited until she had handed Grace her cup and sat down herself before she said, 'Maria, she is going to be married soon. I tell you this?'

'You certainly did,' Grace said tightly as she remembered the pain Bianca's venom had caused.

'So now she will have her own house and her own husband, this. . .friendship with Donato will be no more.'

'There was no friendship of the kind you mean, Bianca.' Grace put down her coffee and met the almond-shaped eyes in which the old hatred was still burning. 'And I'm not sure Maria ever said there was.'

'She did.' Bianca's gaze didn't waver. 'But it is of no importance now, one way or the other. She is getting married and you are returning to England. There is no need—'

'Oh, no.' Grace's voice was too high, but she just couldn't rise to the same cold detachment Bianca was displaying now. 'If Maria said those things then she must retract them, in front of both Donato and myself.'

'What do you mean?' For the first time Bianca appeared ruffled. 'It is all over, finished, and perhaps I misunderstood what she was saying—'

'Then I will find that out when I confront her—with Donato.'

'No.' The calm had only been skin-deep and now Bianca rose, flinging her cup and saucer down so violently that the coffee spilled over the table and floor and the cup smashed. 'I will not have her upset needlessly.'

'Oh, come on, Bianca.' She was sure now. For the first time she was absolutely sure Bianca was lying. It was written in the fury on the lovely face and in the narrowing of the slanted eyes. 'You did all this, didn't you? Not Maria. It's unforgivable—'

'Unforgivable?' It was clear Bianca realised she had

been backed into a corner, that the last gamble to make Grace believe her hadn't paid off, and now she lifted her chin as she stared down at Grace, her expression frightening.

'You talk of this when it should be you begging me for forgiveness? You try to take my place with Madre, you turn Lorenzo against me. I know. *I know.* I am the daughter of the Vittoria house—*me*, not you. And how can Donato love you, really love you, when you let his son die? He was glad when you left Italy.'

'I didn't let Paolo die. It was a cot death—it wasn't anyone's fault,' Grace whispered as she rose to her feet. 'How can you say such things—?'

'And there is me—*me*, who would be a good mother, an excellent mother, but it will not be.' Bianca continued talking as though she hadn't heard her protest. 'There is something wrong here—' Bianca touched the flat skin of her stomach '—that makes it unlikely I can carry a child.'

Her voice had been rising all the time she spoke and now she was spitting the words out of her mouth, her eyes wild with hate. 'And when you let your baby die, it was poor Grace this and poor Grace that—no one talked of anything else. But it is not right that you should have another chance to have more, not with Donato. It is not *fair*!'

'Bianca—'

'And you say I am a disgrace to my husband, that I am not a woman!' Bianca was panting hard now, the words pouring out in a stream that was unstoppable. 'But there are men who can tell you I *am* a woman, that I am very much a woman—'

'Stop it—'

'"Stop it".' The mimicry was vicious. 'Oh, you English! You have no fire, no passion. How could you believe your husband was having an affair, Grace, how could you? Donato—Donato of all people. I could hardly believe even you were so stupid, but it was so easy—so easy and so enjoyable. You thought you had taken my place with them all but I won. I won, did I not? I never share what is mine—you understand this now?'

'Listen to me.' Grace forced herself to stand straight and still. 'I'm sorry if you can't have children, Bianca, terribly sorry—but you never said, so how was I expected to understand? And the last thing on my mind was taking your place in the family.'

'Liar.' Bianca's voice was dripping with enmity. 'I saw you run to Madre that day you left, you know,' she said with an air of slyness that was chilling. 'You did not see me, did you? You thought I had left. But I follow you, I hear what you say. And Madre, she begged you to stay, her precious Grace. And then when you go I get the key from Donato's study and find the note. I knew you would leave one, you see.'

'You took the letter?' Grace asked faintly. But of course. It was the only answer. 'You went into my home and stole the letter?' She had poured out all her pain, her anguish in that letter.

'Such pathos,' Bianca mocked cuttingly. 'How I despised you when I read it. You tried to turn him against me but I was too clever for you. I was always too clever for you. And if you repeat all this I shall deny it, do you hear me? I shall deny it and Donato will believe me. There will be no more babies with Donato, Grace, to flaunt in front of me—'

'*Bianca*.' One word, but the effect of it on the two women was like a thunderbolt as they both turned towards the open doors and saw Donato's tall, dark figure in the opening.

'No. . .' As the colour drained from Bianca's face Grace found her legs were giving way, and sank down onto a chair, the room appearing to spin. 'You should not be here,' Bianca whispered agitatedly as she faced her brother. 'No one was supposed to be here.'

'But I am here, am I not?' Donato said softly. 'And that means it is over, finished.'

'She. . .she is accusing me of saying bad things.' Bianca swung her hand towards Grace as she spoke, her face taking on the innocent, wide-eyed mask she usually adopted in Donato's presence. 'She wants to find an excuse for leaving you and she has decided to put the blame on me. Tell her I—'

'It's too late, Bianca.' Donato took a step into the room as he spoke, his eyes flashing to Grace for a second before they fastened back on his sister. 'I was outside long enough to hear all I needed to hear. It is over— whatever you have done, whoever you have involved, it is finally over.'

'No!'

'*Si*. You need to see a doctor. You are not well.'

'I do not need a doctor.' The mask slipped and then dissolved as Bianca fairly spat the words out. 'I hate you. I hate you all, do you hear me? You think you are so righteous, so noble, ha! You make me laugh with your petty notions of right and wrong. I will do what *I* want. I am answerable to no one—no one!'

Grace was holding faintness at bay by sheer will power. The trauma of the last few weeks and the devastating emotion of the night before compounded by lack of sleep and food were all conspiring to make her lightheaded, but as Bianca glared at her she shut her eyes, fighting the blackness, vaguely aware of a sudden flurry of movement and noise before a pair of hard male arms pulled her close.

'My darling, my darling, it is okay—everything is okay. Can you hear me?'

'Donato. . .'

'Open your eyes, Grace. Look at me, dearest. She did not hurt you?' His voice was ragged with shock and pain, and she could feel his shaking through her own flesh as he pulled her upright and into the protecting confines of his body, pressing her against the hard wall of his chest until she could hardly breathe.

'No, I'm all right. . .' It was all she could manage before the storm of weeping overcame her, her voice a low moan of pain as tears streamed down her face.

And then she was lifted into his arms as he sat down

in the chair she had vacated, settling her on his lap as though she were a small, distressed child and murmuring words of love and tender endearment into the soft silk of her hair which made her cry even more. But mixed up in the pain, the anguish, was the breathtakingly sweet knowledge that it was going to be all right. *It was really going to be all right.*

CHAPTER TEN

IT WAS some long minutes later before Grace struggled to sit up, her face still wet with tears and her hair caught in damp strands across her cheeks.

'Here. . .' Donato brushed away the tendrils with a gentle fingertip before cupping her face and taking her salty lips in a deep, hungry kiss that spoke of his love and desire. But a ghost of the sobs that had racked her body was still with her in tiny muted hiccups, and he rose after placing her gently in the seat, walking across to the large, well-stocked cocktail cabinet and returning almost immediately with a balloon glass filled with a measure of brandy. 'Drink it, Grace, it will help.'

He knew she didn't like the spirit but he held the glass to her lips until she took it from him. 'Come on, straight down.' The fine old brandy made her gasp a little as it burnt a path to her stomach, but Donato was right, it did help, and after another moment or two her breathing had steadied.

He was crouched in front of her, his eyes never leaving her for a moment as she forced herself to speak. 'Bianca?' she asked tremblingly. 'Where is she?'

'I do not know. She ran out of here and I presumed she was going upstairs at first. But then I heard a car start outside, so perhaps she has gone somewhere to calm down.'

'Oh, Donato. . .' As her mouth began to quiver he shook his head, before whisking her into his arms and carrying her out of the French doors and onto the veranda that stretched along the whole of the back of the house, placing her gently into one of the big cane seats dotting the portico.

'No more of that—not now. You are in the sunlight, my love, and I will not allow the darkness to touch you

178

again. We will face this together...if you can forgive me.'

'Forgive you?' For a moment, just the tiniest moment, she thought he was admitting that he *had* had an affair with Maria, and then she pulled herself together, reproaching herself immediately for the suspicion. That particular demon was dealt with once and for all, and she would never doubt him again. And she should be down on her knees telling him so. '*Me*? Forgive *you*? Oh, Donato, it's the other way round. I'm so sorry—'

'No!' His voice was savage but his anger was directed at himself, not her, and as he crouched before her again she saw his face was rent with pain. 'I should have known. I should have understood that you are not capable of listening to casual gossip, that it was something far more sinister than that—something of which you were entirely innocent. But all I could think of were the months apart, when I was going mad without you, the months when you were in England and managing without me. I couldn't manage without you, you see...'

'I couldn't live without you. I couldn't. I just existed—'

She lifted her arms to him and he gathered her up before sitting back in the seat, settling her securely on his lap and kissing her until she had no breath left.

'I love you, Grace,' he said softly. 'I have always loved you and I always will. Nothing you can do or say will ever make me love you less. You are my reason for living, the heart of me. Without you there is nothing. Can you understand this, believe what I say?' He moved her slightly from him so he could look deep into her eyes which were brilliant with unshed tears. 'Do you really believe it?'

'Yes.' And she did, at last. 'Yes, I do.'

'I do not know why we have had to go through this time of desolation—first Paolo's death and then the months apart—but it has made me love you more, not less,' he continued softly. 'This is the truth. When I saw your face as Bianca said those things—'

'It is over now.' She stroked an errant lock of coal-black hair from his brow, her expression tender as she saw the anguish in his face. This must be terrible for him, worse than it was for her. Bianca was his sister after all. 'But I don't understand how you knew I was here. I told no one—'

'Except one very irate parrot.'

'Benito?'

'Benito.' He smiled at her open-mouthed astonishment. 'I never intended to go to the office this morning. I knew I had to talk to you and try to untangle this mess, but when I saw you at breakfast I. . .I did not know how to begin.'

'You didn't?' Her astonishment increased ten thousand times. Never in a million years would she have expected Donato Vittoria to be tongue-tied.

'You still have no idea of the power you have over me, have you?' he murmured tenderly, caressing her face and allowing his touch to linger on the delicate, pure line of her throat before he forced himself back to the conversation in hand with obvious effort. 'I went for a walk in the grounds to clear my mind.' he continued quietly, 'and when I returned I came to find you. Benito was screeching enough to wake the dead—no one could calm him.'

'Oh, the papaw!' She put her hands to her face. 'I forgot to give him the rest of the fruit.'

'That you did,' Donato agreed drily, 'and between his frustration on missing out on his favourite fruit and the fact that Bianca's name had obviously been mentioned more than once, he was more than a little vocal. He repeated your name and Bianca's and enough of what was said for me to understand where you were.'

'And so you came,' she said softly.

'Si, I came.' His voice was deep and rich.

'She said. . .she said she can't have children, Donato. Has Romano mentioned anything to you?' Grace asked.

'Nothing.' He suddenly pulled her to him again with an urgency that met an answering chord in herself. 'But now I have to call my friend, the man who is like a brother to me, and tell him enough to bring him home. I am going to hurt him and I have no wish to do this, but everything can be faced as long as you remain at my side. Bianca...she must be sick, Grace—you understand this?'

'I know, I know. It doesn't matter what she's done, not now we're together again, and we'll get help for her.'

'Oh, Grace...' His mouth devoured hers in an agony of need that told her his pain and confusion and horror were on a par with hers, and she responded fiercely, unutterably glad they had found each other again. 'Are you able to cope with remaining here so we can break the news to Romano in private?' Donato asked a few minutes later, when he raised his lips from hers.

'I want to be wherever you are,' she said shakily. 'That's all.'

'And you will be, my love, from this day forth you will be.'

Romano drove back from Naples in half the time that was legal, and when they heard his powerful Ferrari scream into the courtyard Donato rose quickly, leaving Grace sitting quietly on the shady veranda at the back of the house as he went to meet his friend.

Grace never knew exactly what passed between the two men, but when they came through to her a few minutes later Romano's face was white, and he walked over to her, drawing her gently into his arms for some moments as she stood to greet him. It was an unusual show of affection from the reserved, proud man and it touched her deeply, misting her eyes as they all sat down.

'Grace, what can I say? That you should have been hurt so deeply...' Romano shook his head slowly. 'Donato, too—it is unbelievable. I knew nothing of this story about Maria, although I have been aware for a long time of Bianca's resentment of you. It would have been the same whoever Donato married. She couldn't tolerate

another attractive young female coming into the family—
it is not you personally she disliked.'

'Romano. . .' Grace hesitated, wondering if she should
continue, but Bianca's words had shocked her so pro-
foundly she had to know for sure. 'Bianca said she
couldn't have children; is that true?'

'In a way.' Romano shook his head again, his handsome face set in lines of pain. 'There were tests done
which revealed she needed an operation to have a chance
of conceiving her own child, but the thought of surgery
terrified her, so she convinced herself slowly over a
period of months that there was no hope whether she
had the operation or not. She developed a dislike of all
young women—it became a sickness I could not ignore.
There had been problems before this time. . .'

He shut his eyes tightly for an infinitesimal moment
but didn't elaborate, and such was the look on his face
that they didn't ask him to. But Grace remembered
Bianca's reference to men who could tell her the Italian
woman was 'very much a woman', and she wondered. . .

'Romano, if this is too painful. . .'

'No.' He cut short Donato's quiet voice with an
upraised hand. 'There are things you must understand—
things that I believed must be kept between a man and
wife, things of trust. But now Bianca's actions make it
necessary to reveal the full facts.' He took a deep breath
before continuing, 'When she decided she couldn't have
children things became a hundred times worse than that
which had gone before.'

'Worse?' Grace asked softly.

'Bianca has been seeing a psychiatrist for some time
now,' Romano said flatly. 'Something I insisted on
because I was worried about her, although it made things
between us more difficult. She resented what she saw as
my interference. He was concerned about her mental
state; he sees her infertility as the catalyst for her sickness, not the cause.'

'What is the cause, then?' Donato asked slowly.

'He feels it is some kind of hereditary weakness, but

as she was adopted at birth it is impossible to know for sure.'

'You did not tell me.' Donato shook his head as he looked at his friend. 'Your life must have been a living hell and you did not tell me. Why? I might have been able to help in some way.'

'You could have done nothing,' Romano said quietly, 'and you had enough problems of your own to deal with. If I had known Bianca had a hand in them that would have been different, of course, but I did not. And she is my wife, Donato. "Till death us do part".'

'Oh, Romano. . .' Grace reached out to him, touching his hand with her own.

The police car arrived just minutes later, the two gruff, middle-aged police officers woodenly sympathetic as they told the stunned husband that his young wife had been killed instantly when her car had gone off the road at a hairpin bend. She'd been driving far too fast, according to witnesses at the scene.

No one else had been hurt in the accident, one of them added quietly, which was something to thank God for because the road had been particularly busy at the time.

It was a tragedy, a shocking tragedy. . .

CHAPTER ELEVEN

'WE DID the right thing in bringing Lorenzo away, I know that, but I can't help worrying about Romano.' Grace stretched lazily on the huge double bed as she watched Donato dry himself after his shower, his powerful muscled body causing her heart to beat a little faster despite her anxiety about Romano.

'He is a man, my love. A strong, proud and very good man. He will find the strength to go on and he wants to do it alone. There are times when it does not help to have even the closest friends near,' Donato said quietly as he joined her on the bed.

'And you think this is one of them?' Grace asked worriedly, still unconvinced. 'I worry about him all alone in that big house.'

They had flown out to Tunisia just days after Bianca's funeral, to an enchanting little whitewashed house Donato had rented for several weeks, its garden full of sun-drenched bunches of grapes that were as sweet as honey, and tall green palms and flowering shrubs bordered by eucalyptus, orange and lemon trees.

Lorenzo had fallen in love with the place at once, the shock of his sister's death following so closely on his mother's receding in the new surroundings, and his recovery being helped still more by the joy of finding a friend of his own age in the villa just down the road with whom he ran wild most days, returning when he was hungry or it was bedtime.

'This is one of them.' There wasn't a shred of doubt in Donato's voice. 'I have known Romano all my life and he can deal with it no other way, trust me.'

'I do—oh, I do.' She reached out to him, running her hands over his hard male body, across the range of muscled flesh. 'It's just so awful...'

'It is not just for Lorenzo that I have brought us away,' Donato said softly as his body responded to her touch. 'You know this, *mia piccola*? You needed to escape for a time, to put the past behind you and gain strength for the future.'

'I couldn't think of a better place to do it,' Grace said dreamily, taking pleasure in the hard, hot arousal he was not trying to hide, her love for him so fierce it hurt.

The days in this ancient country had been bitter sweet, the pain and anguish they had left behind in Italy making the time more poignant, more precious for them both.

They had shopped in bustling bazaars and busy souks deep within narrow, twisting streets, had wandered along fine white sandy beaches hand in hand with a crystal blue sea lapping gently at their bare feet, had eaten freshly grilled fish washed down with small refreshing glasses of mint tea, had loved, laughed and sometimes cried.

But, magical though the days had been the nights were better, when they were truly alone, with Lorenzo tucked up in bed in his own room. The long, sweet hours spent in each other's arms were a healing process for them both, the burning passion that took only a touch or a glance to be fanned into a devouring fire more strong, more real than it had ever been in the time before they had parted.

'You do not doubt my love for you?' Donato moved over her, his breathing harsh as their bodies burnt with heat. 'There could never be anyone but you, my love. I still cannot believe I let you suffer so badly, that I was so blind.'

'No, Donato.' She touched his lips with her hand, moving her head slightly to look closely into his dark eyes. 'It wasn't you—it wasn't even all Bianca, really. You were right about me punishing myself for Paolo's death, but I just couldn't help it. I can't really explain how it was except to say I felt I didn't deserve you or such happiness. When it all went wrong it seemed to confirm my subconscious fears, and then Bianca got involved.'

'*Mia piccola...*' His face twisted with pain as he stopped her words with the pressure of his mouth, crushing her to him so fiercely that she could hardly breathe. 'And now?' He lifted his head, his eyes searching hers. 'How do you feel now?'

'Reborn,' she said simply, her eyes wide and clear and showing him all the love and desire in her heart. 'And I know there'll be more children—not to replace Paolo, because he will always be special, closer than my own heartbeat, but others who will be loved for who and what they are.'

He nodded slowly, his face rent with tenderness and love, before stroking her body with soothing, sensual fingers until there was nothing in the world but him. His mouth began to trace the smooth, silky contours of her body, lingering over the secret places until her breath sobbed in her throat and she moaned against him with little sighs, utterly lost in the exquisite timelessness of his lovemaking.

'No more ghosts from the past?' he murmured, his voice husky with desire and relief. 'No more doubts or fears?'

'None...' She couldn't say anything more, her body arching and moving against his as he found the taut peaks of her breasts, the fire inside her so intense as to be a mixture of pain and pleasure. But still he urged her on, taking her to the very brink of satisfaction before drawing her gently back and then resuming his sensuous assault.

'Donato, Donato, please...' She didn't recognise the soft, frantic little whimpers as hers, but when he lifted her to him, possessing her with a completeness that had her shuddering in ecstasy, she cried aloud. He began to move within her, deeper and deeper, until they both transcended into another world where there was no past, no future, merely the glorious, all-consuming present.

They lay entwined for long minutes when it was over, content to be locked in each other's arms without the need for words, their feelings too deep to be expressed. Grace raised herself to look into his dark face after a while and his eyes were waiting for her, the eyes of the Donato only she knew—a different creature from the hard, authoritative mogul of daylight hours.

'What. . .what would you have done if Liliana hadn't died?' she asked softly, not wishing to spoil the moment but finding she had to voice the question that had been hovering in the back of her mind ever since they had got back together. 'I mean. . .it doesn't matter, but how long. . .?'

'How long could I have continued to exist in the nightmare that was life without you?' he asked softly, understanding her need for reassurance. 'I had reached the end of my endurance, Grace, weeks before Madre died. And the name of a certain Dr Penn was appearing too frequently in the reports I had—'

'Jim?' She moved but he wasn't ready to let her go, catching her to him with a fierceness that told her his passion was not spent. 'But he was just a friend, nothing more—you do believe me?' she asked anxiously. 'He was just kind to me, that's all.'

'*Sì*, I believe you.' His voice was very gentle, which made the significance of the words to come all the more emphatic. 'And at the bottom of me, deep within, I knew what was between us could not be broken, but. . .I was ready to kill him, wrestle you from him with my bare hands if necessary. I suffered the torments of the damned every time his name was mentioned. I hated him without even having seen him, this Jim Penn.'

'Donato!' She stared at him, shocked, and he smiled wryly at her expression.

'I am sorry, *mia piccola*, but you asked for the truth and I have to confess that where you are concerned I am the barbarian, *sì*?' he admitted softly. 'I could not share you with another man.'

'I don't mind.' She snuggled into his arms again, her breath quickening as the full thrust of his magnificent manhood made itself known. 'I wouldn't share you either—not with another woman. I'd scratch her eyes out first. Anyway—' she twisted her body to look up into his face '—I want you to want me,' she said passionately.

'Oh, I want you, my beautiful English rose,' he said thickly, easing her silken thighs apart as he invaded the moistness within that was ready and eager to receive him. 'I want you, I need you, I love you far more than life itself...'

And then there were no more words beyond the soft murmurings of their love.

It was later, much later, as Grace was drifting off to sleep wrapped in the warmth and security of Donato's arms, that she heard Liliana's voice speaking the words she had heard so clearly in the dream.

'He needs you, Grace, more than you could ever imagine. It is only when you come home that the healing can begin. Come home, Grace, come home.'

And then she saw it, what Liliana had been trying to tell her. She *was* home. She breathed in the fragrant poignancy of the thought as she allowed her mind to drift into the shadowed world of sleep. Home was where Donato was... *and she was home.*

**Look for these titles—
available at your favorite retail outlet!**

January 1998
Renegade Son by Lisa Jackson
Danielle Summers had problems: a rebellious child
and unscrupulous enemies. In addition, her Montana
ranch was slowly being sabotaged. And then there was
Chase McEnroe—who admired her land and desired her
body. But Danielle feared he would invade more than just
her property—he'd trespass on her heart.

February 1998
The Heart's Yearning by Ginna Gray
Fourteen years ago Laura gave her baby up for adoption,
and not one day had passed that she didn't think about
him and agonize over her choice—so she finally followed
her heart to Texas to see her child. But the plan to watch
her son from afar doesn't quite happen that way, once the
boy's sexy—*single*—father takes a decided interest in *her*.

March 1998
First Things Last by Dixie Browning
One look into Chandler Harrington's dark eyes and
Belinda Massey could refuse the Virginia millionaire nothing.
So how could the no-nonsense nanny believe the rumors that
he had kidnapped his nephew—an adorable, healthy little boy
who crawled as easily into her heart as he did into her lap?

**BORN IN THE USA: Love, marriage—
and the pursuit of family!**

Look us up on-line at: http://www.romance.net

BUSA4

Coming Next Month

HARLEQUIN PRESENTS®

THE BEST HAS JUST GOTTEN BETTER!

#1935 LOVESTRUCK Charlotte Lamb
Nathalie's boss, Sam, was a little the worse for wear when he proposed to her at a party, so she decided to play along and pretend she believed he meant it. And soon she was really beginning to wish he *had*....

#1936 SCANDALOUS BRIDE Diana Hamilton
(Scandals!)
Nathan's whirlwind marriage was already heading for the rocks—he was sure his wife was having an affair with her boss! It seemed the only way to save the marriage was to learn the truth about his scandalous bride once and for all....

#1937 MISTRESS AND MOTHER Lynne Graham
Since separating on their wedding day, Molly maintained that nothing could persuade her to share her husband's bed.... Until Sholto agreed to settle her brother's debt—in return for the wedding night he never had!

#1938 THE LOVE-CHILD Kathryn Ross
(Nanny Wanted!)
When Cathy turned up at Pearce Tyrone's villa in the south of France, he assumed she was the nanny he'd been waiting for. But she knew it was only a matter of time before he found out that she wasn't all she seemed....

#1939 SECOND MARRIAGE Helen Brooks
(Husbands and Wives 2)
Claire would make the perfect bride—everyone said so. But Romano Bellini didn't want his life complicated by a second wife. Curious, then, that the subject of marriage just kept coming up!

#1940 THE VALENTINE AFFAIR! Mary Lyons
Alex had promised her newspaper a Valentine exclusive on Leo Hamilton. And after dogging Leo's all-too-attractive heels, she realized she wanted him as an exclusive, all right—exclusively hers!